LOST INNOCENTS

Victorian England is at the centre of the civilised
world, yet atrocities lurk beneath its enlightened
veneer. Young children are vanishing from their
homes, but the subject of child prostitution is
considered too terrible to contemplate. Virginia
is eighteen, chafing against convention and the
restraints of her privileged position. She devises a
small rebellion, pitted against villains who think
nothing of committing murder, she encounters
greed, cruelty and fear ... and the power of love.

To all the writers of fiction who have entertained and inspired me.

LOST INNOCENTS

by

Jean Rowden

Magna Large Print Books
Long Preston, North Yorkshire,
BD23 4ND, England.

British Library Cataloguing in Publication Data.

Rowden, Jean
    Lost innocents.

    A catalogue record of this book is
    available from the British Library

    ISBN   978-0-7505-3574-8

First published in Great Britain in 2011 by Robert Hale Ltd.

Copyright © Jean Rowden 2011

Cover illustration © Stephen Mulcahey by arrangement with
Arcangel Images

The right of Jean Rowden to be identified as the author of this work
has been asserted by her in accordance with the Copyright, Designs
and Patents Act, 1988

Published in Large Print 2012 by arrangement with
Robert Hale Ltd.

Magna Large Print is an imprint of Library Magna Books Ltd.

Printed and bound in Great Britain by
T.J. (International) Ltd., Cornwall, PL28 8RW

Chapter One

'Virginia!' Her name, as so often on Mrs Kington's lips, was a reprimand.

Turning, Virginia made no attempt to conceal the lantern she had taken from its hook inside the cellar, but she nudged the door with her foot, hiding the basket she had placed just beyond it. 'Did you want me, Mrs Kington? I thought you were resting.'

'I may no longer be your governess,' the woman said, 'but I am charged with being your companion and confidante. Perhaps you would care to tell me what you are doing? If you are not satisfied with the way Mr Willshire performs his duties with regard to Sir Mortimer's wine cellar, you should approach him when he is on duty, not creep behind his back when he has taken the afternoon off.'

'I have no intention of visiting the wine cellar,' Virginia replied. She refrained from adding that while she might be forced to accept her company, Mrs Kington would never be her confidante. In less than a week her cousin would be home, and when he arrived she fervently hoped that the woman would be removed from the household.

'Do you deny what is before my eyes? You were obviously going into the cellar.'

'I have no interest in the wine, or Willshire's duties. I planned to go exploring.'

5

'Exploring?' Mrs Kington's thin face became even more pinched about the mouth. Had the woman still carried the authority of a governess, punishment would already have been decided upon; Virginia would have faced a cold and hungry evening. 'It was your cousin's express wish that you should learn to deport yourself like a lady. By the age of eighteen my previous charges were rarely in need of guidance or instruction. I regret I must consider you my first failure, since despite all my efforts you remain a hoydenish romp. It is to be hoped that Sir Mortimer has no illusions about presenting you at court, for you would certainly disgrace him.'

Virginia flushed. She couldn't tell Mrs Kington the true reason for her sudden interest in the cellars, so she was left with only two possible courses of action: either she could refuse to offer any explanation, or she could lie.

'Well, Virginia? Do you intend to add dumb insolence to your bad manners?'

'When my cousin first brought me to this house, nearly four years ago, he showed me a little of the maze of passages which lead from the cellar,' Virginia said, 'and he told me they might be Roman. My curiosity was aroused during our visit to the museum last week. You have often told me that a thirst for knowledge is a virtue.'

'Not when it involves gallivanting about in the dark amongst the rats and cobwebs! And you know Miss Forswick's opinion of the cellars, who knows but our neighbour may be correct. How would I explain to your cousin if he returned home to find you had caught some terrible fever from the mephitic airs below the house?'

'I confess I hadn't given that a thought,' Virginia said, with a slightly exaggerated sigh. She leant to hang the lantern back on its hook, and closed the cellar door. 'If you wish, I shall abandon my archaeological project, and spend the afternoon in my room.'

Virginia sat staring out of her window; another of the bad habits Mrs Kington had endeavoured, and failed, to cure. There wasn't much of note going on outside, although she saw Mrs Yelding, sister and companion to their neighbour, Miss Forswick, trip lightly across the street; she would be on her way to visit one of her many friends.

The visit to the cellar was to have been made on Mrs Yelding's behalf. Meeting in the haberdasher's, Mrs Yelding had confided that her pet cat was missing. 'Of course, she was approaching her time, and would run off soon, but I fear she has got into the cellar.'

'The cellar?' Virginia had been intrigued. 'Surely Miss Forswick thinks it harbours the plague! Don't you keep it locked up?'

'Yes, but we have a new maid. The silly girl made a mistake, though it was hardly her fault; nobody realized that the key for the broom cupboard was exactly the same as the one to the cellar, and the two doors are next to each other. Maria simply went to the wrong one, and I am very much afraid that my poor cat may have slipped down the stairs.' She paused. 'My sister's hearing is acute. I dare not risk opening the door again, or we'll have her in hysterics.'

'I suppose you must wait until she is out of the

house,' Virginia said.

'But that won't be until Sunday, which is a long time to leave the cat locked up, in her condition. Sir Mortimer once told me that all the cellars are connected, and I was wondering if you might ask your servants to conduct a little search for me.'

Virginia had shaken her head; Willshire, her cousin's butler, was a cat hater. If he laid hands on the kittens they would never see the light of day, and she wouldn't put it past him to despatch the mother cat as well. 'I have a better notion.'

It should have been easy, but for Mrs Kington's sudden appearance. Sighing, Virginia moved from the window to sit at her bureau, taking out the most recent letter she had received from her cousin, to read the final lines once more. She almost knew them by heart.

For the moment I ask that you continue to obey Mrs Kington, although I agree you no longer need a governess, now you have attained the age of eighteen. I expect you to defer to her wishes, particularly in matters of manners and etiquette. Do your best to act as a young lady should, and we shall discuss your future when I am home, which will not be long now.
Your loving cousin
Mortimer Bantry

For the hundredth time, Virginia tried to guess her guardian's intentions for her; he made no mention of marriage, yet what else could be in his mind? Sir Mortimer was out of the country so much of the time, perhaps he would be unwilling to stay long enough to help her find a suitable

8

husband; the prospect of him giving Mrs Kington *carte blanche* to arrange matters was enough to make Virginia quail.

Sir Mortimer had taken care of Virginia since she was twelve years old, when her parents died in India. He had hurried across the world to fetch her as soon as the news reached him, thus becoming her saviour and hero. An inveterate traveller, her cousin had succumbed to the temptation of taking an indirect route back to England, and Virginia had greatly enjoyed journeying in Sir Mortimer's company. They had been accompanied by Mrs Connolly, acting as her governess; being gay and light-hearted, that lady hadn't spent much time on formal education. It had been a great blow when the cheerful widow was replaced by Mrs Kington on their return to London, and an even greater one when Sir Mortimer announced his intention of setting off on his travels again, this time to South America, after less than six months in England, and adamantly refused to take Virginia with him.

The afternoon dragged into evening; dinner was eaten in silence, and she made her excuses and retired to her room long before she really wished to go. A powerful resentment had been growing within her since the disagreement with Mrs Kington and Virginia came to a resolve. Mrs Yelding's concern for her cat was not Virginia's foremost reason for venturing into the cellar, and she had no interest in Roman antiquities.

Her exploration must be put off no longer; she would begin her undertaking that very night. Sitting by the window, so there was no chance that she would fall asleep, Virginia waited for the clock in the hallway to chime twice, then crept from her room. When Sir Mortimer first showed her the cellar, he had told her a story of a kitchen boy who had gone down there alone, many years before, and vanished. Despite all efforts to find him, the boy was never seen again. Virginia wasn't quite sure she believed this tale, but she had packed a long skein of thread in the basket, along with spare candles and the matchbox from her cousin's desk. Cook had asked no questions when asked to provide her with the remains of a joint of mutton, a chipped saucer and a small jug of milk.

The basket was still where she had left it. Virginia's hands trembled a little as she lit the lantern, but her nerves steadied as she made her way carefully down the steps, pausing at the bottom. The silence here felt oppressive; even the faint scuff of her shoes on the flags seemed too loud, and she couldn't bring herself to call out to the cat. Standing by the door to the wine cellar, Virginia peered into a narrow arched entrance, framing total blackness.

Tying one end of her thread to the handle of the wine-cellar door, she set off; carefully unwinding the yarn, the dim light from the lantern casting shadows that leapt wildly about her. A small shiver ran down her back; the unseen echoing spaces felt more alien than anything she had encountered while travelling the wider world with her cousin.

Within a few yards an opening yawned on her left; it should take her beneath Miss Forswick's house. The passageway looked dark and discouraging. Virginia took out a spare candle and lit it, letting a few blobs of wax drip on the stone by her feet and using them to fix the candle to the floor. Careful that the thread came nowhere near the flame, she went on; it would be a comfort to look back and see the little glimmer of light.

The tunnel, narrower than the first, soon came to a dead end. There was an unpleasant odour here, and Virginia wrinkled her nose as she retreated, rewinding the thread as she went. Having returned to the candle she resumed her exploration, until she located another turn to the left. This time the passage opened into a large chamber, where wide columns supported a low vaulted ceiling, rather like a church crypt. It was impossible to tell whether there were any exits without venturing further; the place was a maze, just as her cousin had warned. For a moment Virginia's resolve weakened; she could return to her bed and nobody would ever know she had been here.

It wasn't concern for Mrs Yelding, or the cat, which sent her on, but the thought of her cousin. If he deserted her again, if he made no permanent arrangement for her future before he resumed his travels, then she would take desperate measures rather than be left in Mrs Kington's hands for every hour of every endless day.

Virginia skirted around a pillar, and was rewarded by the sight of a set of steps. Mrs Yelding had questioned the maid, Maria, about what she had seen when she opened the forbidden door, and passed this information to Virginia. Some previous occupant of Miss Forswick's house had thrown a heap of jumble down the stairs, and Maria had described it in some detail.

11

As Virginia advanced she made out a table with a leg missing, a small dresser, badly smashed, and a very large mirror with a broken frame. She had come to the right place.

'Puss?' she whispered tentatively, creeping closer to the steps. She pulled the remains of the mutton joint from the basket. 'I've brought you some food, Puss, and milk.'

Dust lay thickly upon every surface, and wide strands of cobweb lay like the worn rigging of a wrecked ship, over the heap of lumber. A broken table lay tilted across the top of the stairs, and Virginia thought it very unlikely that even a cat could have passed that way without knocking it over. She sniffed. The air was stale, but she could detect no scent of cats. Mrs Yelding must be mistaken; her pet was probably hiding in the house, and would emerge triumphant with her kittens when she was ready. However, it wouldn't hurt to leave her gifts, just in case. Virginia poured out the milk, and left it with the meat, by the bottom step.

Feeling she had done all that could be expected of her, Virginia considered she was free to pursue her own purpose. She wound up the thread, and returned to the lighted candle, where she abandoned the basket, putting a spare candle and the matchbox into her pocket.

A few yards further on, the original passage was blocked, and Virginia was forced to turn into a winding tunnel which soon split into three. Again she chose to turn left, but by this time her sense of direction had deserted her. Without the thread she would have been hopelessly lost; the lantern showed nothing but the dirty stone flags beneath her feet. Virginia was growing cold, and a little discouraged. She refused to believe the kitchen boy had perished; he must have found a way out, but where had he gone?

She stepped into another large gallery, where the roof was again supported by crumbling stone pillars. There was a subtle change in the nature of the darkness ahead of her. Far away, something was twinkling, bright one moment, almost vanishing the next. Virginia's pulse quickened; this could be what she sought. She held the lantern behind her back, and at once the distant light seemed to brighten. Fumbling in her pocket to make sure of the matchbox, she lifted the lantern once more. With fingers that shook more with excitement than fear, she opened the glass, and blew out the flame.

Virginia focused on the little gleam that danced tantalizingly before her eyes. She put down the lantern, tying the thread to its handle so she could be certain of finding it again if the light before her vanished. Unravelling her clew with great care, she crept towards the flickering glow, one furtive step at a time. She came to a broken door hanging from a frame, much of it rotted away. When she reached out a hand to touch the remaining planks their edges crumbled to dust, swirling into the still air, and the light vanished. Virginia's heart pounded painfully beneath her ribs. After a moment of fearful hesitation she took a wary half-step and the glimmer reappeared, shining some distance ahead of her, not a candle as she had thought, but a lamp; she could smell the oil.

Scarcely daring to breathe, Virginia kept her

13

gaze fixed upon that intriguing glow. It came through a hole in a brick wall. Some of the bricks had tumbled, allowing the light to reach her from the next chamber, and more looked ready to fall, sagging towards her as if the merest draught would send them to the floor. Virginia halted, as near as she could come to the opening without risking a turned ankle on the heap of rubble.

As Virginia stood, nerves stretched to breaking point, a spider dropped onto her neck. She came perilously close to screaming, but her breath stuck in her throat, which was fortunate; from the other side of the wall came the sound of a footstep, followed by a cough.

'Faugh, there's a stench down here.' It was the voice of a gentleman, sounding as if he stood right at her side. For one bizarre moment Virginia thought the words were being addressed to her, but before she made a reply, the man spoke again.

'Come now, don't try playing dead,' he said, 'you would be wise to talk to me. Mudd will be back soon, and he'll not be gentle. Why were you following him?'

There was no response. Hardly breathing, Virginia leant closer to the bricks.

'Dammit, are you deaf?' The smooth-voiced gentleman was beginning to sound impatient. 'Before he kills you, Mudd will make you talk, be assured of that. Why not save yourself a great deal of discomfort?'

Virginia Bantry prided herself on being a modern young woman; thanks to her upbringing she was no milk and water miss. Certainly she wasn't in the habit of swooning, but for the first time in her life she thought she might faint. If she hadn't been aware of every step that had brought her here, she might have believed she was trapped, not in the cellars below Lucas Place, but in a nightmare. As the dark wall before her seemed to shimmer, she reached to steady herself. With a slight grating sound something shifted at her touch, and Virginia froze; her hand was trapped, and blood oozed warmly from her little finger.

Her heart began to pound painfully beneath her ribs as the full horror of her position hit her. If she moved, the wall might collapse, revealing her presence to the smooth-voiced man on the other side. Turn and run, and he must surely hear her. She was held as fast as a fly in the web the spider was spinning in her hair.

Chapter Two

Somewhere a door opened. The sound echoed through the underground chambers, and when it slammed shut again the light beyond the gap in the wall brightened. Virginia glanced back; the candle she had left alight was far away, there was not even the faintest glow to suggest which way she had come. The thread she had spun out drew a darker line upon the dusty stone, vanishing in the gloom beyond her feet. Escape to the real world lay there, if only she could summon up the resolve to free herself.

Virginia stayed where she was, peering at a

patch of uneven floor; beyond lay a slab of stone, standing higher than the dusty flags surrounding it. Somebody began to descend a set of steps, heavy footfalls resounding loudly in the silence.

'It took you long enough.' It was the man she had heard before, only now his tone was petulant. 'We don't have all night.'

'Blimey, y'r honour, you told me to look in ev'ry corner, an' tha's what I done. There wasn't nobody wiv 'im, tha's fer sure. You want me to send 'im down to the fishes?'

'Not yet, you fool. I need to know who he is. Maybe he came alone, maybe not. So far he's not said a word, I'm not even sure he's heard me.'

'I 'ad to give 'im a good tap, or 'e'd 've scarpered. Wriggly little cove 'e was.'

Virginia forced herself to remain still as the newcomer approached. He looked huge, made grotesque by wildly gyrating shadows; a second lamp swung in his great fist. She had the impression of rough working clothes. A ray of light flowed across the back of Virginia's hand and she drew in a sharp breath, ready to pull away. Her luck held; the lantern passed her by, leaving her in obscurity once more.

'Playin' dead, is 'e? I'll give 'im a tweak somewhere tender. That works in the ring, ev'ry time.' There was a pause, and then a rough muttered curse and the sound of a blow.

'The man's unconscious, you blockhead. Did you have to hit him so hard?'

'Wasn't no 'elp for it, y'r honour, 'e'd 'ave bin long gorn else.'

'He might not come round for hours. Damn

16

you, Mudd, I need the wretch to talk. He may have friends who'll make trouble if he disappears.'

'Wasn't my fault, y'r honour,' the ruffian whined. 'If I 'adn't give 'im a good un, 'e'd 've 'oofed it. Reckon 'e'll slip away quiet, easy as pie. Why don' I tip 'im in?'

'I have to know what brought him to us, you dolt. Somebody may have been told what he planned to do, and we want no more busybodies. See if you can rouse him.'

'It'll be one o' the little molls 'e's after, tha's all, some little chit of an armful 'e took a fancy to. T'ain't only the gentry wot likes 'em young. Lemme tip 'im in, y'r honour, an' no 'arm done,' the rough voice wheedled. 'Blokes don' go blabbin' to their pals when they're runnin' arter little 'uns; 'e won't be missed.'

'I said, rouse him.' The gentleman's voice was cold and menacing. 'If you can't obey orders there are others who will.'

'I'll wake 'im, y'r lordship,' the ruffian said hastily. 'Jus' gimme a minute.'

Virginia flinched at the sound of flesh striking flesh, followed by a groan.

'There, y'r honour, 'e's comin' round. Give 'im 'alf a mo' an' 'e'll be ready to sing like a linnet. See, I tol' y'r lordship I'd fix 'im.'

'Let's hope he's not a reluctant songster.' The man's bad temper seemed forgotten now that he had what he wanted. 'All right, Mudd, there should be news of the delivery by now, you'd better get back up and see if there's a message. If he hasn't told me what I want to know by the time you return, you may loosen his tongue for him.'

The man addressed as Mudd passed across Virginia's sight again, though she saw no more than a thickset shape running by. 'I'll not be long, y'r honour,' he said, hurrying up the steps, 'E'll sing for me, don't you worry.'

There was a brief silence before the gentleman addressed his captive once more.

'I know you are conscious, don't think you can fool me by pretending to be unfit to talk.' He gave a cold laugh. 'Of course, that may come, once Mudd gets his hands on you. Tell me why you were spying and perhaps I'll let you live, but you'd better speak up quickly. You heard how eager he is; the oaf likes his work, and he doesn't always know when to stop.'

Virginia longed for the captive to answer and she mouthed a silent prayer. If he was wise and did as he was bidden, perhaps murder might still be prevented. The seconds dragged into minutes, feeling like hours, but as far as she could hear the prisoner made no sound.

'Answer me, what brought you here?' his captor demanded. There was a slight noise, as if he had taken hold of his prisoner and shaken him. 'If it concerns an item of merchandise we may be able to come to some arrangement.' He dropped his voice, the gentlemanly tone at odds with the words that he spoke. 'I deal in human lives every day. It wouldn't be the first time I'd been forced to remove somebody who interfered with my business – it can be done with a minimum of fuss.'

Still no answer came. The smooth-voiced gentleman laughed. 'Perhaps you expect to be rescued. You have friends, family. Perhaps you

18

told them what you were up to, and you are relying on them to call in the police. Don't fool yourself. All things have a price, and in London the law may be bought quite cheaply. Should I wish it, there are police officers who will help to cover our tracks; nobody will ever know how your body came to be found floating down at Greenwich.'

Virginia shuddered. There was a silence so deep she could almost believe the man was speaking to himself. A part of her still wanted to run, to escape; this would be a good time, while the huge ruffian was out of the way, but she couldn't do it. She could not abandon this poor unfortunate. If she ran back to her cousin's house, to whom could she turn? Sir Mortimer wasn't expected for a week. Mrs Kington was well versed in matters of etiquette, but this situation would be far beyond her. The servants might be roused, and a policeman summoned, but according to this smooth-voiced villain the law could not be trusted.

Virginia could guess how those in authority would react if she tried telling such a far-fetched story; she was eighteen, little more than a girl. They would label her an hysteric and call for a physician. She tried to imagine telling old Dr Norris that she had been a witness to kidnapping and threats of murder; it was quite impossible.

'Come, man, don't you value your neck? What brought you here?' Again there was no reply, and the questioner sighed in exasperation. 'Speak to me now or I turn Mudd on you,' he said. 'He's on his way, don't you hear the door?'

Heavy footsteps clattered down the stairs once more. Virginia had made no move. For her, as for the helpless victim of these evil men, the moment to act had gone.

'The boy came,' Mudd said, as he hurried past the gap in the wall. 'I was to tell you Mrs 'Ardwin is on 'er way, wiv two pieces o' merchandise. Be 'ere in ten minutes, 'e says.'

'Only two of the little dears? That Hardwin woman is losing her touch. I wanted this finished first. Hoist open the trap, Mudd, let him see where he's bound if he doesn't talk.'

Virginia held her breath as the big man came back into her sight. He bent low over the slab of stone that stood just above the level of the floor, and grasped a metal ring at its centre. When he straightened, a vile stench rose with him. Virginia could never recall encountering such a smell. For the first time she wondered if Miss Forswick was right; this reek was powerful enough to start a dozen plagues. She recoiled, and then froze as a brick shifted with a slight grating sound.

'Whassat?' Mudd spun around. Virginia closed her eyes, screwing them tightly shut. She was a child again; if she couldn't see the one who sought her, she must be invisible.

We've disturbed a few rats.' The gentleman sounded amused. 'Even they must find that odour less than sweet. Come, man,' he added impatiently, 'move this fool a little closer, let him enjoy the full benefit of that charming perfume, then do what you must.'

There was the sound of something heavy being dragged across the stone floor. 'Talk, damn y'r eyes,' Mudd growled, and Virginia blenched at the sound of a blow.

'Careful, Mudd. If his body gets washed up it must look as if he's had an accident.'

'Not to worry, y'r honour, I knows what I'm doin'.'

Virginia could make nothing of the sounds that followed this declaration; there were faint creaks, as if of wood under some strain. A dull popping noise came next, followed quickly by another. The victim still spoke no word, but she heard a sharp indrawn breath. She tried to clench her fists, and felt fresh blood flowing from her trapped finger.

'Speak, damn you! Why did you come here?' The gentleman was pacing in agitation. His voice and his hurried footsteps were almost a relief to Virginia, since they hid those other vile sounds she couldn't block from her ears.

Mudd was breathing noisily now, as if he was expending some effort, and she heard another gasp, a groan, but the prisoner still refused to speak.

'Enough!' The gentleman stopped his pacing. 'We have no more time.'

'C'n I send 'im fer a swim?' Again came the scrape of wood on the stone floor.

'I didn't say that. We'll leave him to think. He'll be safe enough left here for an hour. We had better settle with Mrs Hardwin and inspect these new arrivals. Let's hope they are easier on the eye than the last she brought us.'

Virginia caught a glimpse of the two men as they strode to the steps, the lanterns sending shadows circling wildly around; the gentleman was considerably smaller than Mudd.

The door closed on total darkness. She could run now, fly back to her room, hide beneath the bedclothes and pretend that none of this had happened. It was a terrible temptation. There was no sound from the captive, not even a breath. Had he fainted? Or died? If he was dead then there was truly nothing to be done.

Precious time was passing. Almost without coherent thought, the decision was made. Virginia fumbled in her pocket. It took three attempts to strike a match, but at last there was light.

Once she had pushed the tottering wall, there could be no easy escape, but Virginia hesitated no more than a second. The bricks tumbled noisily to the floor amid clouds of choking dust. Suppressing the urge to cough, she waited, listening intently. There was no angry cry or rush of footsteps from above. As soon as the dust had cleared enough to allow her to see the way, Virginia wriggled clumsily through the gap, holding the candle before her.

Hot wax dripped on to her fingers as she struggled to her feet. As she had guessed, the prisoner was tied to a chair, his body slumped forward; since he hadn't heard the crash that heralded her arrival Virginia assumed he must have lapsed into unconsciousness.

Between her and the captive lay the gaping hole in the floor, with the stone flag tilted open above it; now and then an unpleasant gurgling sound issued from below, along with the stench that seemed to get worse with each passing moment. Virginia edged around the noisome shaft, pinching her nose, yet unable to resist the temptation to lean forward and peer into the turbid depths. Far down, she caught a faint fluid movement.

The man stirred as Virginia approached. His head began to lift and she steeled herself, expecting to see a face terribly damaged by Mudd's brutality. A pair of dark eyes met hers, widening in disbelief as they ranged over her, from tangled dusty hair, over her dishevelled robe and down to her scuffed slippers. Apart from a split lip that was bleeding freely, the young man appeared unharmed.

'Where did you come from?' The captive looked around wildly, scanning the darkness behind her. He looked much younger than she had expected, no more than two or three years older than she.

'Never mind that, we may not have long.' She could almost hear the ticking of a clock inside her head, counting off the seconds before Mudd and his master returned. Putting the candle down with care, Virginia bent to the nearest of the knots, where the young man's left wrist was tied to the arm of the chair. She recoiled with a gasp of horror; three of his fingers were swollen and badly misshapen, obviously broken. This was what Mudd had done to him.

Hands trembling, Virginia forced herself to focus on the rope, fearful of inflicting more pain as she teased the knots undone.

'Wait. If you untie the other hand first I can help,' the young man said urgently. Obediently Virginia moved to his right side, relieved to see that this hand was undamaged, and once she had released his wrist it only took him a moment to untie the other. Virginia stepped around the chair to tackle the rope that was fastened behind him, fumbling in the shadows. There was more evidence of Mudd's ministrations here; blood oozed from a wound on the back of the young man's head, matting his dark hair.

'Can you get up? Are you able to walk?' Virginia queried, as the last rope dropped clear. By way of reply he staggered to his feet, his injured hand tucked inside his jacket.

'Careful,' Virginia warned, pulling him away from the hole in the floor. 'Come along, we must hurry.'

He resisted, staring into the filthy spate. 'Wait,' he said. 'How did you get in here?'

'From my cousin's wine cellar.'

'Your cousin? Are you saying you live here? In this house?'

'No. There's a great maze of passages, I have no idea how far I've come. I was looking for a cat,' she added inconsequentially, tugging at his arm. He was staring down the shaft as if mesmerized by the filthy water. 'Please, they could be back at any moment.'

'And when they do they'll be looking for me,' he replied. He began to push the chair towards the opening. 'They'll be on our heels, unless we provide an alternative explanation.'

'Oh,' Virginia breathed, 'I see. You really think anyone would choose such an end?'

'Maybe not,' he replied, 'but it's all we have. Perhaps they'll think I was struggling against the ropes and fell in by accident.'

She nodded and grasped the other side of the chair. Between them they propelled it to the pit and pushed it in. The terrible reek that was released brought Virginia close to retching. As she

24

backed away Virginia trod on one of the ropes; she gathered them up and tossed them after the chair.

'Perfect. All I have to do is vanish as completely,' the young man said.

Virginia picked up the candle to lead the way, squirming swiftly through the gap between the bricks. He tried to follow, but that simple undertaking almost defeated him. Even with all the loose masonry removed, the hole was barely large enough for a man to squeeze through, and the passage couldn't be made without putting weight upon his wounded hand. After several agonizing minutes he lay halfway through, unable to go either forward or back, his face ashen and beaded with sweat.

'I'm sorry,' he said, 'you'll have to help me.'

'Tell me what I can do,' Virginia said instantly, dashing hot tears from her cheeks with the back of her hand.

'Take hold of my left arm at the wrist and pull,' he replied. 'Don't worry,' he added, 'it's only the fingers that are damaged, you'll do me no harm.'

'But it will hurt,' she protested.

He forced a grin, his lips white. 'It hurts already. My dear impossible saviour, you've been so magnificent, don't fail me now.'

Somehow it was done. Feeling as sick and pale as the young man looked, Virginia left him slumped against the wall and did her best to replace the bricks that had been dislodged; the repair wouldn't stand close inspection, but when she had finished the hole was barely large enough to allow a rat to leap through.

'Come along,' she urged, pulling his right arm

around her shoulders, 'it's a bit of a walk, but we need to get out of this maze before they come back.'

He murmured some protest, trying to pull free. 'I'm bleeding. It will soil your clothes.'

Virginia felt an hysterical laugh rise to her throat. 'Don't be ridiculous, I'm filthy already, and look at my hand. What does one more splash of blood matter?' She supported him as they made their way back through the passages, gathering up the clew which showed them the way; Virginia was amazed to find how many twists and turns she had made. She recovered the lantern, and was soon snatching up the candle she had left near Miss Forswick's cellar.

'You left quite a trail,' the young man mumbled. He was leaning upon her more heavily with each step. Lurching, staggering, they made their way past the locked door to Sir Mortimer's wine cellar, where Virginia untied the thread. How they managed the flight of stairs she never knew, but at last they stood swaying in the deserted hall, almost the whole of the fugitive's weight now supported upon her aching shoulders.

'Not much further.' The front parlour, a small dingy room that was rarely used, was only a few steps away. As Virginia turned the handle and thrust the door open, the young man suddenly became a dead weight; they pitched forward together, sprawling on the floor.

Chapter Three

The hiss of the lamp and the occasional scratch of pen on paper sounded loud in the small room. Jocelyn Roper's office looked on to the street, and sometimes he could see the tobacconists opposite; tonight when he lifted his head nothing was visible but the halo of fog around the gaslight, a few feet from the window.

From downstairs Roper heard a thump as a door was closed at the back of the offices; the press had faded into silence some half-hour before; the next edition of the *City Examiner* would soon be on London's streets. The building in which Roper sat had the appearance of a dwelling, a twin with the one next door which was his home. Having the offices of his journal adjacent to his house was an arrangement he found both economical and convenient.

Putting down his pen and abandoning his work, Roper listened, taking in the distant sounds of the city in its predawn lull, waiting for something closer, beginning to feel concerned. After a while he lit his pipe, sucking hard and then adding a great cloud to the fumes already filling the room; they rivalled the murk out of doors. He was waiting for a visitor, but that wasn't the cause of his underlying anxiety; the message he'd received earlier had not been exact regarding time.

If questioned, Roper would have denied feeling

27

uneasy, but it would have been untrue. His nephew should have returned by now. Of course, if he was on the trail of something worthwhile he might not be home for hours or even days. There were many who said Simon was a chip off the old block, the son Jocelyn had never had, and it was true the young man had a grip like a terrier once he took hold of a story.

Chewing at his pipe, the proprietor of the *City Examiner* gave his head a little shake. He was in danger of thinking about the circumstances which had placed his nephew in his charge. He mustn't become morbid. Roper believed in honesty, morality and plain speaking; he had convinced himself long ago that he had no time for sentiment.

The rap at the door was barely loud enough to make itself heard. Unhurriedly, Jocelyn Roper propped his pipe in its customary place against the inkwell, pushed back his chair and rose, making no attempt to hurry. His head of fine white hair, added to an air of calm benignity, gave him the look of a kindly schoolmaster. For a man so tall and spare, and of such an active mind, he moved with a strangely slow gait; the knock was repeated before he reached the front door.

'Don't you keep a servant?' The man on the doorstep walked in without awaiting an invitation. He wore his top hat low over his forehead and a silk scarf wrapped around his nose and mouth, yet Roper knew the identity of his visitor at once. He had been in his profession too long to betray surprise, but he was disconcerted; the message had suggested he was awaiting a government official, some anonymous flunkey, not one of Her Majesty's ministers.

Somewhere close by a church clock chimed four. 'I sent my man to bed hours ago,' Roper said, stepping back to allow his guest to enter the office before him, 'Since this is hardly the normal time to be making calls I assumed the matter was to remain confidential. Even the city's rogues are mostly off the streets by this time.'

The newcomer gave him a sharp look, as if he suspected this comment might have been a gibe at the expense of his character, rather than a simple observation. 'I was kept late at the House,' he replied. 'I trust the hour is not inconvenient to you.'

'A newspaper editor keeps unconventional hours,' Roper said, 'sometimes just as late as Westminster.'

His visitor scanned the room, his gaze resting for a moment on two doors in the opposite wall. 'We cannot be overheard? What I have to say must not leave these four walls.'

'Perhaps you would care to inspect the closet?' Roper invited, lowering himself into his chair and waving a hand at the door on the left, looking even more like a kindly headmaster indulging a favoured pupil.

With another of his darting mistrustful glances, his guest strode across and opened the door his host had indicated, revealing a tiny room filled with books and papers. Not waiting for permission, he moved to the right. The second door gave on to a narrow passage.

'That leads to my parlour,' Roper said easily. 'There is nobody at home apart from the married couple who act as my manservant and housekeeper, I would rather you didn't wake them. The woman suffers from dyspepsia when her routine is disturbed, and on such occasions she becomes a haphazard cook, producing quite inedible food, although at other times her meals are as good as any served at the best hotels. I only refrain from writing about this phenomenon for fear that she might take umbrage and leave. I dislike domestic upset.'

His visitor was still standing, and Roper gestured at the chair on the other side of the desk. 'You'll find that seat reasonably comfortable; it has accommodated several of your fellows over the years, though not often so early in the morning. I trust you had no trouble finding your way here. I have a belief that the fog becomes even more impenetrable at this time of day, but that may only reflect my dislike of the dark. This is a particularly disagreeable hour, don't you think? It has been suggested that both murderers and suicides particularly favour the period between three and five.'

'May we forgo the niceties of making polite conversation and come to the point?' the man said abruptly, making no effort to hide his contempt; he was known to have a fine idea of his own importance and by now he probably rated the editor as a chattering fool.

Roper offered his visitor a slight smile; men were far more likely to be indiscreet when in the company of those they despised. 'Forgive me, I am told I talk too much. The floor is yours.'

'You must know the reason for my visit. Your current campaign is libellous. The allegations you have made must be retracted, and there must be no more of this nonsense. If your suggestions weren't so ridiculous you would be charged in a court of law, but it would be folly to encourage your flights of fancy by bringing them more widely to public attention.'

'I have named no names, so I can hardly be guilty of libel,' Roper responded reasonably. 'And in what way do you find my articles fantastical?'

'In their subject matter,' the man replied. 'Your imagination has run away with you. In the last week you have moved so far into the realms of sea-monsters and three headed giants that there are those who doubt your sanity.' He took a crumpled sheet of newsprint from his pocket and read aloud, his sharp features drawn into an expression of intense distaste. *'I write of matters far removed from the healthy physical relationships between the sexes, and on this occasion I am not concerned with the normal practice of prostitution, which is surely as old as mankind itself, and probably as indestructible. Any person of compassion must share my outrage, however, when unnatural acts are perpetrated upon mere infants, children as young as six or seven years of age. Not content with the normal release for their most basic urges, there are some men with bizarre and cruel appetites. Even now, as we approach the end of the nineteenth century, and consider ourselves rulers of a civilized empire, there are rogues in London procuring young children for wealthy and seemingly respectable men, for most evil and immoral purposes. There are houses of ill-repute where, hidden from prying eyes, mere infants suffer a life of terror and degradation.'*

The man looked up, glaring at Jocelyn Roper. 'Such things do not happen in England. You

31

condemn our society, and in doing so you criti-
cize our government. These editorials indulge in
the basest kind of sensationalism.'

'On the contrary, I have clear evidence that
these things happen every day, in London, and
elsewhere in this country. Unscrupulous people
steal these children, or, in some cases, buy them
under the guise of an indenture into service,
which is maybe even worse. The parents are left
unaware that they have sent their offspring into
the worst kind of slavery.'

'That is nonsense. Are you saying that a child's
labour cannot be bought? Can we not hire
servants? A poor man has the right to dispose of
his daughters in whatever way he sees fit, and
what of the brats who are born to whores?'

'They may well follow in their mothers' footsteps,' Roper conceded. 'That doesn't make it
right. They are so young! What of the loss of innocence; do we see nothing wrong in debauching
infants barely weaned from their mother's breasts?
A child was recently rescued from the house of a
procuress, by merest chance, and she was judged
to be not yet seven years old. It is difficult to learn
the exact circumstances of her abduction from one
so young, but I have no doubt that she was
kidnapped. Had she not been found, she was to be
the plaything of two wealthy men, respected
gentlemen with children of their own, whose lives
couldn't be more different from those of the poor
unfortunates whose cause I have espoused.'

'I say again, this is nonsense,' the other man said,
a slight flush suffusing his face. 'You can have no
proof, because there is none. Such things do not

happen.' He shook the piece of paper, brandishing it under Roper's nose. 'The ravings of a madman might be dismissed, if you had gone no further, but what follows is even more outrageous. Let us proceed to the full depths of your folly.' His eyes flickering rapidly down the columns of newsprint, he read on. *'In recent months this evil trade has increased, making London its centre. Children are being abducted and sold; once entered into a brothel they cannot escape. If I did not believe that the ordinary folk of this fair city are ignorant of these matters, if I did not believe that they will, when informed of the truth, insist that these crimes must be stopped and the perpetrators punished, I might despair of all humanity. If those in power had no knowledge of these atrocities, they can no longer plead ignorance. Will they act? Do they care sufficiently to protect the innocent and pursue the guilty?'*

'I see nothing wrong here,' Roper put in. 'Even now I am gathering further proof–'

'Lies!' his visitor hissed. 'All lies. And you leave the worst until last.' He stabbed a finger at the paper and read aloud once more. *'At present these crimes continue unchecked. The police do nothing; some of them take bribes, others turn their backs, and I must conclude that their lassitude is condoned by the government. Must we also conclude that men whom we respect, men of influence and power, are amongst those who perform evil acts upon innocent young girls, children of such a tender age that they are not yet old enough to leave their mother's knee? Let us hope not. Let us hope they are merely ignorant of the facts. Let us hope they are as horrified as I am at this wickedness. Let us hope they will act to stop it.'*

The minister threw the offending paper on to the desk. 'Do you deny that your aspersions are nothing but damned libel?'

'I do,' Roper replied mildly. 'It can hardly be libellous when I name no names.'

'There are no names. These things do not happen. You have cast a terrible slur upon Her Majesty's Government. Were it not for our wish to draw no further attention to your calumny, we would take you to court and force you to retract this vicious attack. We insist on your assurance, here and now, that this subject will be pursued no further.'

Jocelyn Roper leant back in his chair, steepling his long fingers and leaning his neatly bearded chin upon the tips. 'I am afraid I do not understand. In what particular have I caused such offence?'

'*Men of influence and power,*' his visitor quoted. 'I fail to see how that could not apply to Members of Parliament. You may have steered away from direct libel, but you come far too close. This must stop, or you will face the consequences.'

The newspaperman shook his head. 'You say I am indulging in fantasy; that I must not be taken seriously. If this is the case, why are you so concerned?'

'Don't play games, Roper. You have exaggerated a rumour in order to sell your worthless sheet. There are thousands of guttersnipes adrift in this city, and it may well be that some of them take up the oldest of professions. Girls become bawds, like their sluttish mothers. What matter is that to any of us? Fathers sell a child's labour to feed the rest of their family; who are we to say they are wrong? It has always been so. The right of individuals is paramount in our society; it is essential that Englishmen remain free to act as they see fit.'

'Women have no rights,' Jocelyn Roper replied bitterly, 'and girls have less than none. You are saying they can be mistreated with impunity. But no matter how unwilling people are to hear the truth, these things happen, each and every day. Small children are being sold into sexual slavery. During the course of my investigation I have un-covered an organization luring country girls to London with promises of honest work, only to deliver them into the hands of ruthless whore-mongers. Admittedly, these children are close to becoming women, being maybe twelve or thirteen years of age, but they have not reached the age of consent. The methods used to procure those who are too young to enter regular employment are even more reprehensible.'

Roper leant forward, eager to emphasize his point. 'It would be a simple enough matter to af-ford these children some protection. Any girl be-low the age of fourteen who was found in a brothel could be removed; she could be offered shelter, maybe even education, until such time as she can be found decent employment. The church would help, and there are admirable charities, set up to assist women who repent of their immorality.'

The minister's eyes were hard, his expression unyielding. 'I did not come here to debate with you, but to warn you of the folly of pursuing this matter any further. You have maligned some of the most powerful men in the country, Roper, and your interference will not be tolerated.'

'Interference? An interesting choice of word.' The editor reached for his pipe; his long fingers gripped the stem hard as he struggled to control his feelings. 'And do I detect a threat? What a shame there are no witnesses of this meeting.'

'This meeting never took place,' the other retorted. 'I repeat, you would be wise to give up this campaign. As to the truth or otherwise of your allegations, that is immaterial.' He stood, scowling down at the man behind the desk. 'You must be aware of the forces ranged against you.'

'Indeed I am.' Roper too rose to his feet; he topped the politician by a head. 'For centuries the nobility, and those who aspire to their ranks, have exercised a seigniorial right, and they are reluctant to let it go. Where they lead, others follow, and so these evils continue. Those not actively involved turn a blind eye. As long as this wickedness is allowed to go on, England is besmirched, undeserving of its place at the head of the civilized world. That is my last word, and I bid you good night, sir.'

When he was alone once more, Roper sank into his chair. He had not intended to come so close to losing his temper. He sucked on his pipe, cocking an ear towards the house; going to the door he opened it, listening to the silence on the other side. The boy would not have retired to bed, having seen the light still shining in his office. 'Simon?' he queried, keeping his voice low, but assured that it would reach to the parlour at the far end of the passageway. There was no response.

It was too late to seek sleep. By now the de-

36

livery of today's *City Examiner* would be under-
way. Jocelyn Roper rose, and went through to the
back of the building. His arrival in the print room
was greeted with little ceremony, the business of
getting the journal onto the streets being well in
hand. Grimes, the typesetter, his own work finished for the night, came across to his employer.

'There was a lad here with a message for you,
sir, he wouldn't give it to me. I told him you
weren't to be disturbed, and he said he'd wait.
He'll be out the back I expect, making a nuisance
of himself among the delivery boys. Do you want
to see him?'

'Yes, thank you, Grimes. No mishaps tonight?'

'No, sir, she ran sweet as a nut the whole way
through.'

As he waited for the man to fetch the messenger, Roper felt a tiny jolt of excitement. In a
few hours his latest editorial would be the talk of
London. His enemies at Westminster would
receive his answer to their threats, loud and clear.

The boy was brought to him, a redheaded
urchin clutching a battered black cap to his chest.
'I'm told you have a message for me.' Roper said.

By way of response a grubby hand delved
inside the cap and brought forth a scrap of paper.
'The geezer said you'd give us a tanner,' he said,
keeping a tight hold on this offering as Roper
reached to take it.

'None of your cheek,' Grimes said, laying a
heavy hand on the boy's shoulder.

'I doubt if sixpence was mentioned,' Jocelyn
Roper said calmly, taking out his purse and ex-
tracting two pennies. The exchange was made

and the messenger was thrown out by Grimes, with a cuff round the ear for his trouble.

Roper took the paper to the nearest lamp. It was creased and grubby, the hasty pencil lines scrawled upon it being barely discernible. Roper scowled down at the message; it was nonsense. One below the other, four words had been written; as far as he could make out, they said *Mud Comb Lucan Peace*.

Chapter Four

Virginia struggled up from the floor. Pausing on her knees she held her breath, expecting to hear cries of alarm from upstairs, but none came. After a while she rose to her feet, and having lit the oil lamp, she dragged the young man further into the room so that the door would close.

Her situation was still perilous, although now it was her reputation she was putting at risk, not her life. For a respectable unmarried woman the two were almost the same thing. Reflecting ruefully that it was a little late to start regretting her actions now, Virginia let herself out of the room, treading silently towards the kitchen. There was work to do; she must try to get her fugitive on his feet and out of the house before his presence was discovered.

It was dark in the hall, and darker still at the back of the house. Suddenly something blocked Virginia's way, a black shape, appearing to rise from the ground at her feet. As a squeak of alarm escaped Virginia's lips, a candle stub, held in a small grubby fist, was lifted from below. Puffing slightly, a little maid climbed the rest of the way up from the coal hole, manhandling a large bucket. Several scuttles, already filled, were ranged along the passage.

'Beg pardon, miss,' the child said, ducking her head in apology, and scurrying to move the obstacles so Virginia could pass by.

'Whatever are you doing here at this hour?' Virginia whispered.

'I have to get the coal up the backstairs before Agnes starts work, miss.'

'Since you're here you can help me,' Virginia said decidedly. The child was a stranger to her, small and thin. Her frock was reasonably clean, but far too big, and patched in many places.

'But I have to take the coal up, miss,' the child replied. 'Mr Willshire says I have to do it before I start any other jobs.'

'I've not seen you before,' Virginia said.

'No, miss. Mr Willshire says I'm not a fit sight. I work in the scullery, miss. Please, miss, you'll not tell him you saw me?' she begged, her eyes huge in the gloom.

'Of course I shan't, if you don't want me to. What's your name?'

'Emily, miss.'

'Well, Emily, this morning you must help me. Fetch a jug of hot water at once.'

The girl looked quite terrified, as if Virginia had asked her to commit some heinous crime. 'I can't, miss. The coal has to be ready for Agnes so she can light the fires. I mustn't be late, miss.' There was something akin to hysteria in her voice. 'Please, miss, let me call Agnes. She's the upstairs maid, it's her place to help you.'

'No, that won't do. There's nothing to be afraid of, Emily, it will only take a few minutes, and then you may return to your normal duties.'

'Please miss, I dassen't. Not when Mr Willshire made himself so plain.' There were tears on the child's cheeks. 'Maybe once I've took up the coal. I'll be quick as I can.'

With sudden decision Virginia picked up a scuttle in each hand, surprised at their weight, which made it hard to straighten her back. 'I could fetch the water myself, but there's something I can't manage without your help. Come on, we'll do this first.' Ignoring the girl's terrified protests she led the way up the narrow back stairs.

A few minutes later, with smudges of coal dust added to the stains on her robe, and her hands full with sponge, towels and smelling salts, Virginia returned to the front parlour, followed by Emily who carried the jug of hot water. The lamplight spilled out as the door was opened, and the little maid gasped. Looking down, Virginia saw the state of her clothes; she hadn't realized how much her fugitive had bled. 'Hush,' she said, 'it's nothing. There's somebody here who's been hurt, I'm sure you aren't afraid of a little blood.'

'No, miss,' Emily said faintly, staring now at the young man, sprawled untidily at their feet. 'He don't look very comfortable, miss.'

'I couldn't lift him on to the couch on my own.'

Even between the two of them it was a struggle,

but at last he lay on the cushions. Virginia studied the young man's face. He was rather dishevelled, but his hair had been tidily cut, and his moustache and side whiskers, if a little thin owing to his youth, were very neat. In the cellar she had given no attention to the captive's clothes, and now she could see him clearly she was puzzled; his jacket looked as if it belonged to a labourer. The cuffs were frayed and a button was missing. It was strange then, that the right hand lying upon his chest showed no signs of manual labour, while his shirt was made of clean white linen and looked almost new. She smiled to herself, her interest piqued by this mystery; the few words he had spoken had already convinced her that he was no common working man.

Virginia sponged the invalid's split lip, and washed the wound on the back of his head. He moved a little under her ministrations, not waking up, but shifting so that his left arm came free from where he had tucked it inside his coat.

'Oh, miss,' Emily said, holding the water for her mistress, 'look at his poor hand!'

Reluctantly Virginia obeyed. The broken fingers were badly swollen; they needed the attentions of a physician, but how could that be done, when his very presence in the house must remain a secret?

'That looks awful bad,' the maid observed.

'Hush, I'm thinking.' Virginia had the beginnings of a plan. 'Stay here, Emily, I shan't be a moment.' She ran up the stairs to her room and changed into a clean robe. Carrying the soiled garment back to the parlour she pushed it into Emily's hands. 'You have to wash the blood out.

I can manage here on my own, so once that's done you may return to your work, but come and warn me a few minutes before the other servants come down.'

'Yes, miss.' The child nodded. 'I can read the kitchen clock. I'll come at a quarter to six.' She ducked in a quaint attempt at a curtsy and left, closing the door silently behind her.

Alone with her refugee, Virginia was free to study him. The young man was stirring, his sound hand closing into a fist, and his head turning a little on the cushions. There was a black stain upon the index finger of his right hand; she wondered if he might be a clerk. Her gaze moved to his face, and she found herself staring into a pair of deep blue eyes.

A shock ran through her, every part of her body suddenly wide awake and tingling. She had listened to many sermons about carnality and the evils of sexual desire; in a split second she came to understand the root of the preachers' warnings. An excitingly wicked heat was coursing through her veins, bringing sensations that were totally new; between one breath and the next, a deep instinctive knowledge had awakened. Those who claimed humans were related to the beasts had been right after all.

Had the stranger sat up and pressed his lips upon hers, in that moment Virginia would have welcomed his salute, and returned it, with no thought of her good character. The realization brought a deep flush to her cheeks. 'Are you feeling better?' she said, thankful to find that her voice didn't betray the turmoil of her heightened emotions.

'You!' His gaze did nothing to calm Virginia's racing heart. 'You're the angel who came into my nightmare and saved my life. But you're real! Or am I still dreaming?'

With an effort she lowered her eyes from his. 'You're awake, and I assure you I'm totally human,' she said. When she risked glancing at him again he was studying his surroundings with a puzzled look on his face.

'How did I get here?'

'Don't you remember? Mudd gave you a nasty knock on the head.'

'I don't remember much, except being some-where cold and dark. Before that – I was follow-ing somebody, was that Mudd?' He touched the back of his head and winced. 'There was a man, a smooth devil. He spoke like a gentleman, but I believe he intended to kill me. You can see why I'm baffled, I rather expected to wake up dead.' The young man spoke lightly but there was just the faintest tremor in his voice. 'I'm sorry, this is no fit subject for your ears. And you have no chaperon. I don't understand where I am, or how I came to be here alone with you. That at least I can remedy.' He tried to push himself upright, collapsing with an involuntary cry of pain as he leant on his injured hand.

'Please, take care,' Virginia begged. 'In order to explain your presence we have to employ a little subterfuge. I'm sorry I can't send for a physician yet. Just be patient a while.'

The young man was beginning to look agitated.

'But it's the middle of the night; think of your reputation. Is there nobody you can summon?'

'Please, don't fuss,' Virginia replied. 'There's no risk. Take time to collect your thoughts. You've had a very unpleasant experience.'

'I barely recall,' he said distractedly. 'It still seems more like a nightmare than reality. I'd got myself into the most frightful fix, and you appeared from nowhere like some seraphic guardian. You set me free. But where did you come from?'

'The cellars are a positive labyrinth. Don't you remember being down there?'

'Yes,' he replied, an expression of dawning comprehension on his face, 'perhaps I do.' He frowned. 'You mentioned a cat.'

'Oh,' she gave a shaky laugh. 'That was why I went into the cellar in the first place; my neighbour's cat is missing, and she thought it might be hiding down there with her kittens. Our butler doesn't like cats, and if he finds them they'll be drowned.'

The young man shuddered. 'As I would have been, if you hadn't come to my rescue. That part is coming back. We crawled through a hole in a wall, or rather you dragged me, and then you sealed it up again. And there was a door which fell away to dust when you touched it, and that seemed like another miracle, like the parting of the waves. You can see why I thought you were an angel.' The look in his eyes was making Virginia feel uncomfortably warm again, and she pushed herself quickly to her feet, moving to the other side of the room.

'Then I was a very frightened angel,' she said.

44

'Perhaps I should introduce myself. I am Virginia Bantry, cousin of Sir Mortimer Bantry. You are in his house, by the way, although he's away from home until next Wednesday. There's nobody here with me but the servants, and my companion, Mrs Kington.'

'My name is Simon Roper,' he said, 'and I am forever in your debt.' Tucking his left hand inside his jacket, he rose slowly to his feet. 'I can't allow you to compromise yourself in this way, Miss Bantry, I am sure you acted as you thought best, but I must leave.'

'And risk walking into Mudd or his employer in the street?' She barred his way to the door. He was swaying as if he might collapse at any moment. 'Sit down before you fall and do yourself more hurt. Tell me how you came to be held prisoner by those two men.'

'I can't remember exactly.' He lowered himself back onto the sofa, though with evident reluctance. 'I work for my uncle, Jocelyn Roper, at the *City Examiner.* I was seeking information to help with a series of articles, and my enquiries brought me into the company of those ruffians. I beg your pardon, but the subject of my enquiry isn't fit for your ears.'

'I am not one of those delicate insipid females who swoon at the mere mention of blood,' Virginia protested crossly. 'I heard a little of what was said in the cellar. I believe I am capable of putting two and two together.'

'I'd rather you didn't,' Simon Roper said, his pale cheeks taking on a pink tinge. 'Please, I fear I can't speak further on this matter, not to you. I owe you a great deal, but for now the very best service I can perform is to leave as quickly as possible.'

'Nonsense.' Virginia glanced at the ugly French clock on the mantel. 'We have ten minutes, and then I'll be able to send for the doctor. I told you, I'm no milk and water miss. I have travelled in India, Africa and Europe, and I am not a fool. From what I heard, I imagine those men are procurers, trading in women who are to engage in prostitution.'

Simon Roper looked astounded, staring at her as if lost for words.

'Well?' she prompted. 'I have seen things that would send most young ladies into a fashionable swoon, but I assure you I am not easily shocked. Come, tell me if I am right. Unless you are too squeamish to utter the words?'

At this gibe his lips curved, but the slightly dazed look had gone from his eyes, and there was something different in them as he replied. 'Very well, Miss unshockable Bantry. You are half right. The men are procurers. But they do not deal in street women; they cater for more exclusive tastes. They kidnap young children and sell them.'

'Children?' Virginia echoed faintly. The little room seemed to contract, and his face, now showing the utmost concern, appeared as if in a dark mirror. She took a faltering step back to sink onto a chair. A distant memory, shrouded in a dim red light, came back to her; it was a dreadful shock, for she had worked hard to banish those images from her mind.

'Miss Bantry!' Simon Roper bent over her. 'I

am so sorry. Please, forgive me, I shouldn't have told you.'

'Nonsense.' She lifted her chin and gave herself a little shake. 'Your answer surprised me, that's all. I never imagined such terrible things could happen in England.'

'That is why they continue unchecked,' Roper said soberly. 'It is too wicked to be thought of, so people deny that the crime exists. Now, you must let me leave.'

To Virginia's relief there came a light tap at the door. 'There's no need. Dr Norris can be sent for. He lives nearby, next to the church we attend.'

'Which church would that be?' Simon asked, disingenuously.

'St Joseph's, at the end of Elderman Road,' she said, her own intentions equally and unashamedly transparent. 'I rarely miss the morning service on Sunday.'

Warily she opened the parlour door to usher him into the hall, where Emily stood waiting. Virginia put a finger to her lips, lowering her voice. 'In a moment I shall pretend to let you in from the street, and then I shall raise the alarm. Emily, this will be the first time you have seen either myself, or this gentleman, is that understood?'

'Yes, miss,' the little maid nodded, a sparkle of excitement in her eyes.

'Miss Bantry, I fail to see...' Simon Roper began, but at that moment footsteps could be heard on the back stairs, and with Emily's help, Virginia drew back the heavy bolts and threw open the front door. There was no time for more than a quick glance outside; a man in workman's clothes had just walked into Lucas Place from Newscombe Street, but he showed no interest in her appearance at the door, and otherwise the neighbourhood was deserted. Virginia thrust the bewildered Simon backwards onto the step.

'My dear sir,' Virginia cried loudly, 'I saw the attack from my window and came down at once. You are hurt!' She turned as Agnes came hurrying from the back of the house, a curious Cook peeping from behind her. 'Agnes, how fortunate that you are up! You must rouse Mr Willshire. A terrible thing has happened. I woke early and looked out, and I saw two ruffians assaulting this poor man. I fear they have done him some serious hurt.'

Bowing his head so the servants couldn't see the smile that came unbidden to his lips, Simon Roper addressed his rescuer. 'Forgive me, madam,' he said, 'for this intrusion, but I took a knock on the head, and it has left my brain a trifle addled. I'd be grateful if you could spare me a drink of water.'

'Of course. Please, you must step inside.' By this time the whole household was awake. Mrs Kington was coming downstairs, and Agnes had reappeared with the butler.

'Virginia!' Mrs Kington was outraged. 'All this commotion. Whatever are you doing up and about at this hour? Who is this man?'

'I am sorry, Mrs Kington. I could see no alternative to rousing the servants. This gentleman was attacked in the street.'

Mrs Kington looked Simon up and down, taking in his bare head and disreputable jacket, obviously finding little there to merit the title of gentleman. He was leaning weakly against the

48

doorpost, half in and half out of the house, while keeping his broken hand tucked out of sight against his chest.

'My deepest apologies, madam,' he said, attempting a small bow, 'you see me in a state which is considerably to my disadvantage.' His accent and choice of words were greatly at variance with his shabby appearance. 'My name is Roper, Simon Roper. Two rogues attacked me, perhaps meaning to have my purse. I was foolish enough to resist, and was rewarded for my folly. Forgive me for intruding. I shan't trouble you further.'

He pushed himself upright and turned, but the attempt was too much. His cheeks took on a startling pallor; he would have fallen if Willshire hadn't stepped forward to support him.

'Really, Virginia, look at his clothes,' Mrs Kington hissed in her charge's ear. 'What were you thinking of'?'

'I was thinking that my cousin believes in acts of Christian charity,' Virginia replied boldly, 'and that he would always help those in need. Did not Reverend Porter preach about the good Samaritan only last month?'

Mrs Kington was momentarily silenced, then with a sigh she nodded at the butler. 'It seems we have a guest,' she said, her expression still sour. 'Mr Willshire, I would suggest that you escort him into the front parlour. Please send for Dr Norris. And see that this *gentleman* is not left alone. Agnes, Cook, the excitement is over, kindly attend to your duties. Virginia, return to your room at once, how many times have I told you not to rise so early. Have you no thought for your complexion?'

Chapter Five

There was barely time to rumple the bed and hide
the fact that it hadn't been slept in, before Mrs
Kington came to join Virginia in her room. 'How
did you come to be awake at such an hour?' she
demanded, hurrying to put a hand on her
charge's forehead without waiting for an answer.
'I fear you are feverish, you have an unhealthily
high colour. Get back into bed immediately. This
is most inconvenient, today of all days, when I
had arranged to spend the afternoon and evening
with Miss Cardew.'

'I don't feel unwell,' Virginia said, 'but perhaps
a little overheated, that may have woken me.
Wasn't it fortunate I looked out of the window?
That poor man might have fainted on our step.'

Mrs Kington made no comment, her face regis-
tering displeasure. 'I shall fetch you a posset,' she
said, 'your nerves have been unnaturally excited.'

Virginia nodded meekly, though her heart
rebelled, knowing she would not see Simon Roper
again before he left. While Mrs Kington went to
prepare her remedy, she rose swiftly and stared
into her mirror. No wonder the older woman had
concluded that she was unwell; above flushed
cheeks, her eyes shone brightly back at her from
the glass. Virginia pressed her hands to her face.
She had never felt less like an invalid, nor so alive.

Once she had obediently swallowed the con-

50

coction prepared for her, Virginia was ordered to spend the rest of the morning in bed. Since that meant she would be left alone with her thoughts, she made no protest. Shortly after, she heard Dr Norris arrive, and ten minutes later she was at her window again. It was reassuring to see Simon walk to the doctor's carriage unaided. A tall, soldierly man was holding the doctor's horse, saluting as he was rewarded with a few coppers. As they drove away he dodged between the shrubs in the centre of the place, crossing to where a cart was just drawing up at the house opposite. Obviously he hoped for similar employment with the carrier. Virginia suddenly realized she had seen him before: he had come from Newscombe Street as she pulled Simon in off the doorstep.

Looking down at Lucas Place, the dark passageways that ran beneath the houses seemed suddenly unreal. Virginia recalled something her cousin had told her, a memory of his own youth; seeing her interest in the cellar, he had confided that when the drains had been dug along the street, no trace of the underground maze had been found. Wherever her wanderings had led, she had remained on this side of the road.

Virginia returned to bed, content to stare sightlessly at the ceiling and dream the hours away, full of the hope that Simon Roper would be at St Joseph's on Sunday. As she grew sleepy Virginia's imagination roamed, and strange unsettling emotions ran through her; again she experienced that burning need, that wicked and betraying response of her body. How could a man she barely knew cause such powerful and sinful feelings? And why were they so very appealing? A sound from the rooms below roused her to full wakefulness; the burning heat of desire turned to guilt.

The thought of sin and bodily passion turned her mind elsewhere; an older nightmare had resurfaced when Simon Roper had made his shocking revelation.

It had been an oppressive day, hot even by North African standards. Walking through a bazaar with her cousin and Mrs Connolly, she had stepped aside for a few seconds, seeking shelter from the sun while Sir Mortimer bartered with a carpet seller. As she stood beneath a porch, fanning her face, the door behind her had been snatched open. Whirling round, Virginia had found herself looking into the terrified eyes of a naked child. As the girl balked, finding her way blocked, a large man, wearing no more than the child, swooped down from the shadowed interior and dragged her back inside.

In the brief second before the door was slammed shut, Virginia saw what lay beyond: the man and child weren't alone. She had been little more than a child herself; Virginia's mind had rebelled, so horrifying was the scene, and when Mrs Connolly came to link arms with her and scold her for lagging behind, she walked on in a daze, hardly hearing the woman's words. Never once, in the years since, had she mentioned the incident to anyone. To learn that such evils existed here, in London, had been like the thrust of a knife to her heart, reawakening all her old fears.

Simon and his uncle were crusading to rescue the poor girls he had been so reluctant to speak about, children like that poor infant long ago. Somehow she would find a way to help. His cause would become hers. Refusing to let herself be sidetracked by thoughts of dark-blue eyes, she tried to recall the name of the woman who had been mentioned by Mudd and his master, the one bringing the *merchandise*, but without success.

There were just four houses on this side of Lucas Place, but Virginia only knew Miss Forswick and Mrs Yelding who lived next door. A reclusive old gentleman lived in number three, next to Miss Forswick. At the end, since Major Brand left, number four was rented out to a new tenant each year. Beyond that came the junction with Newscombe Street. Mrs Kington refused to allow Virginia to take her daily walk in that direction, because of the men who hung about near the mews. It seemed a more suitable place to harbour men like Mudd, but his master was a gentleman, and unlikely to live above a stableyard.

Unable to come to any useful conclusions, Virginia returned to a happier reverie. If the weather was fine on Sunday morning she might contrive a few moments of private conversation with young Mr Roper. She wrote the scene in her mind, imagining what they might say to each other. Thus pleasantly occupied, she fell asleep with a smile on her face.

Mrs Kington was reluctant to leave her charge alone that afternoon, but Virginia was eager to persuade her to visit Miss Cardew as she had planned. 'I shall occupy myself quietly, writing in my journal and working at my tapestry,' she declared.

With some show of reluctance Mrs Kington agreed to go. She instructed Cook to serve boiled fish for Virginia's evening meal, in deference to her charge's supposedly febrile condition, and then with a final admonition to Virginia not to tire herself, she left.

Greatly relieved, Virginia sat by the window and watched Mrs Kington climb into a cab. When she turned back to her tapestry, she found Willshire standing in the doorway.

'I have to go out on business in connection with Sir Mortimer's return, Miss Bantry,' he said, with a slight inclination of his head. As always, the butler's manner was correct, even deferential, yet they both knew that with her cousin away, Virginia had no power in the household. 'Agnes has been instructed not to admit any callers, in accordance with Mrs Kington's wishes.'

'Thank you, Willshire,' Virginia replied sweetly, acknowledging the implied criticism of her actions that morning, and replying with a little barb of her own. 'I have no doubt the household will survive very well in your absence, as always.'

As soon as the butler was out of the house, Virginia went down to the kitchen.

'Miss Virginia,' Cook greeted her with a smile, 'I'm just making the sauce to go with the meal Mrs Kington ordered for you.' She winked, reaching for the spice box. Virginia had missed the exotic foods of her childhood when she was brought to London, and Cook had gone to great trouble to recreate her favourite dishes. Having worked for the Bantry family for forty years, Cook was not in awe of the formidable Mrs Kington, and she had been a good friend to Virginia during her first lonely months in England.

'Thank you.' Virginia sat on a stool by the stove. 'I met the new maid this morning. She seems quite bright, but she's terrified of Willshire.'

'Most girls are,' Cook replied. 'Emily does well enough, though I doubt she'll stay any longer than the last. His high and mighty lordship is hard on her. He told her he wanted to see his face in the scullery tiles when he got back.' She put away the spices and came to sit opposite Virginia. 'I expect she'll run off soon like that other little monkey. I don't know that this house is any worse than a hundred others, but we never seem to keep a kitchen maid more than a year. There's times I think of looking for another position myself, with Sir Mortimer being away so much.'

'I couldn't blame you.' Virginia sighed. 'I wish I could leave.'

'It won't be long before you find yourself a nice young man,' Cook said consolingly, leaning forward to pat her hand. 'Only make sure your husband will let you manage the household. And pray he doesn't waste his time gallivanting around the world without you. Don't you go falling out of the frying pan and into the fire.'

Virginia laughed. 'I'll try not to. I was thinking earlier about our neighbours. When the major's wife was alive they used to give wonderful parties, do you remember?'

'I do. Mrs Brand was a lovely lady. We used to have gatherings below stairs, too, at Christmas and Easter. Nearly every house in the Place would be empty those nights.'

'Did the old gentleman from number three come? I don't remember him being there.'

'Mr Parkin? I don't know that he did. There was a son, Mr Jeffrey; he was always invited to the parties if he was home, but that might have been before your time. Old Mr Parkin, he's not been outside in ten years. That must be a sad sort of a house.'

'I never saw anyone coming or going there,' Virginia remarked. 'Not like the Brands'. There were always people in and out.'

'Yes, poor Major Brand, it was a hard blow when his wife died, Lucas Place isn't the same since he left. Even Mrs Ross isn't at number four now. She always hoped the major would come back.'

'Did she leave?' Virginia was surprised. 'I thought she kept house for the tenants.'

'So she did, except this time. A week after the new gentleman moved in, she was gone. It was awkward I suppose, if he brought his own staff.'

'Do you know the man's name?' Virginia asked, her heart suddenly beating a little faster. Suppose the smooth-voiced gentleman was the newcomer at number four? It would explain his eagerness to dispense with Mrs Ross's services; she had been a great gossip. 'I don't believe I've ever met him.'

'He's Reverend Solcott.'

'Reverend? He's a clergyman?' Virginia blurted out. This was a disappointment; she'd already decided that this man was the most likely villain.

'What's wrong with that?' Cook replied.

'Nothing,' Virginia said hurriedly, 'It's strange we haven't met him at St Joseph's.'

'Perhaps he goes to St Jude's, or the Abbey.'

'I'm surprised you don't know,' Virginia said teasingly, 'You always know what's going on in Lucas Place; it's the only way I find out anything interesting.'

'Hmph. Are you saying I'm a gossip?' Cook rose, turning her back and returning to her work.

'Of course not. A bit of idle chatter does no harm,' Virginia wheedled.

'There's nothing much to tell. I did hear the gentleman has a ne'er-do-well brother, who stays in the house from time to time.'

Virginia's eyes widened. This was promising; Reverend Solcott might be innocent, but not his black sheep of a brother. 'What else do you know about number four?'

Cook gave her an old-fashioned look. 'Not much. The only other thing I know is that the butcher's boy got a clip round the ear from Reverend Solcott's groom. But that's not surprising, he's a cheeky little devil.'

'Is the groom called Mudd?' Virginia asked eagerly.

'I don't know. And I can't see what business it would be of yours either. For shame, Miss Virginia, have you nothing to keep you busy? I've got work to do, even if you don't.'

Virginia returned to her needlework, but she couldn't settle. Going to her writing desk, she drew out a blank sheet of paper and pondered over it for a while. She would find some way to deliver a note to Simon. If only there was more to tell. Old Mr Parkin at number three couldn't possibly be suspected, and she'd heard nothing to suggest that his son had returned home. Number four Lucas

Place must have access to the cellar, but Reverend Solcott didn't sound a very likely villain. Chewing on her lip, she felt a little more hopeful of the mysterious brother, and the groom who had made himself unpleasant to the butcher's boy.

Writing to a young man, particularly one she wasn't supposed to know, was totally unacceptable behaviour. Virginia's chin tilted up and she dipped her pen into the ink. With a flourish she wrote his name at the top of the page.

'And at what time did you eventually condescend to return home?' Jocelyn Roper demanded sternly.

His nephew, stooped low over the basin on the washstand, didn't immediately turn round. 'I didn't want to disturb you, sir,' he said, his voice a little muffled as he pressed a towel to his face.

'Disturb me!' The editor of the *City Examiner* was tired, and his temper was short. 'You absent yourself when you are supposed to be gathering vital information for me,' he said, 'you send an incomprehensible note, then creep into the house like a felon. It is nearly midday. Didn't it occur to you that I may be concerned for your safety?'

'I'm sorry the note made no sense,' Simon replied, his back still turned to his uncle.

'Perhaps you would care to explain it now. And have the goodness to face me, sir,' the older man barked.

Simon obeyed, throwing the towel onto the washstand, and trying to tuck his bandaged hand inside his jacket.

'My dear boy...' His uncle took a step towards him, his temper instantly forgotten. 'Have you been in a fight? What happened to your mouth? And your hand?'

'I'm afraid I got a little too close to a certain Mr Mudd,' Simon said.

'Mudd? So that was what your note referred to, a man's name. But *Lucan? Peace?*'

'Lucas Place.' Simon said. 'Admittedly I was a little rushed. It was meant to request that you came to join me there. Was the writing so terrible?'

Wordlessly, Jocelyn took the scrap of paper from his inside pocket and gave it to him. It looked as if the boy who had delivered it had first ground it into the gutter. 'Mud, indeed,' Simon said, his lips quirking into a smile. 'I'm truly sorry, sir.'

'*You're* sorry?' Jocelyn looked at his young disciple. 'I never thought you would be running the risk of encountering physical violence. I shouldn't have allowed you to go alone.'

Simon decided not to mention that he had come close to losing his life; his uncle might prohibit him from any further part in the investigation. 'Then I doubt if I would have learnt anything. As it is, I know we're on the right track. The merchandise is stored in Lucas Place, or very close by, though it seems a very respectable neighbourhood. There is a mews in the next street which might warrant further investigation.'

'Is your hand seriously hurt? Has it been properly tended?'

'I saw an elderly physician who assures me it will mend in time. I'm sorry I distressed you, sir.' It didn't seem the moment to mention the involvement of the charming Miss Bantry; he would save that for later, along with the full story

59

of his adventure, once his uncle had been mellowed by a good dinner and a glass of port. 'I believe I heard the gong. Shall we go down?'

Through the whole of Friday and Saturday, Virginia spent every spare moment sitting by her window, determined to find something of consequence to convey to Simon Roper on Sunday. Not once did she see any man who looked big enough to be Mudd as she remembered him; perhaps the horror of the scene in the cellar had made him appear larger than life.

The tall, upright man who had held the doctor's horse could be seen walking past the house quite often; he might work at the mews, and pass by on some regular errand, or perhaps he was there for some more sinister reason. He could be in league with Mudd, lurking in the street to make sure nobody took too much interest in the kidnappers' affairs.

Late on Saturday afternoon a small closed carriage drove out of the yard behind number four, returning an hour later; whether it had an occupant or not, Virginia couldn't tell. The driver was a large man, but she couldn't see his face under his wide-brimmed hat; she had caught no more than a glimpse of Mudd in the cellar anyway, so it was doubtful she would recognize him. However, the incident was enough to renew her curiosity about the tenant at number four; just because a man wore clerical black, he was not necessarily a saint.

On a sudden impulse, Virginia decided to make a call. She had climbed to the attics earlier in the day, in the hope of seeing further than her neighbour's garden, but she had been disappointed; now it occurred to her that the rooms occupied by Miss Forswick's servants might allow her a wider view. Having made an excuse to Mrs Kington, Virginia invented a tale to tell Mrs Yelding as she walked up the steps to the house next door.

'The church?' Mrs Yelding looked a little puzzled. 'I don't think you will be able to see it from here.'

'I'm not speaking of St Joseph's,' Virginia replied, 'but there is a fine tall spire which is half hidden by another building. I thought if I could see it more clearly I might discover which church it belongs to. Don't you think it would make a pleasant excursion, to take a walk there together, some day when the weather is warm?'

'It may not be in a suitable kind of neighbourhood,' Miss Forswick warned. 'Some fine churches are stranded amongst poor properties.'

'I believe this one is near the park, for there are large trees quite close by. It will surely do no harm to find out.'

'No, of course not,' Mrs Yelding said. 'I expect you are eager to find ways to make the time go more quickly, waiting as you are for Sir Mortimer's return.' Ignoring her sister's slight sigh of disapproval, she led the way out of the drawing room and upstairs.

From the highest window on the side of the house closest to number three, Virginia made a pretence of studying the skyline, expressing profound disappointment that she could see no sign of the elusive spire.

'What a shame. Never mind, my dear, we need

no particular reason to take a walk. I should be very happy to take a stroll with you, any afternoon. The park is always pleasant.'

'Thank you, Mrs Yelding, that is very kind. Perhaps we could go on Monday.' Virginia said, looking at the view closer to home; the stableyard behind number four was hidden by trees, which was disappointing. 'Poor Mr Parkin's garden looks rather neglected,' she remarked.

'Indeed. Look, though, he has had the rear entrance cleared. The stables have been disused for years. I cannot imagine that Mr Parkin intends to make use of his carriage, it must have mouldered away to a heap of dust by now. Perhaps young Mr Jeffrey is home.'

Virginia nodded thoughtfully. Clergyman or not, she still favoured Reverend Solcot as the most likely villain in Lucas Place, unless it was his brother, but perhaps Jeffrey Parkin should be on the list of suspects; she had learnt something to add to her letter.

Chapter Six

At last Sunday came, and Virginia prepared for the short walk to church with such alacrity that she was ready a full quarter of an hour before her companion, despite having dressed her hair with more than usual care before pinning on her hat. 'You look quite charming,' Mrs Kington remarked, with rare approbation. 'But I fear your colour is still a trifle high.'

'I feel well,' she replied hastily. There were times when she thought Mrs Kington loved to thwart her; it would be disastrous if she were forced to stay home. Virginia's fingers tightened on the chatelaine purse hanging from her wrist. The little bag had once belonged to her mother, and she rarely used it, but today it had a special purpose; through the fabric she could feel the note she had penned with such care.

'You are excited at the prospect of Sir Mortimer's return,' Mrs Kington said tolerantly. 'A lady doesn't show her emotions so openly, Virginia, please make an effort not to overexcite yourself, there are only three more days to wait. Come, it is a pleasant morning; it will do you no harm to linger in the churchyard for a few minutes before the service.'

Virginia nodded meekly. Mrs Kington would hope to meet Miss Cardew; that might well provide an opportunity to deliver her note, as long as Mr Roper did not come late. The fine weather had brought many of the congregation out early; Mrs Yelding hurried over to Virginia to confide that the kittens were safe in Miss Forswick's scullery.

'They were in the house all the time,' Mrs Yelding said happily, 'the clever cat found the perfect place, and she has already brought them out to show me. Come and see them soon,' the old lady added over her shoulder, trotting away to catch up with her sister.

As Virginia looked about her, despairing of finding the only person she had any interest in seeing, she noticed the vicar entering the vestry.

There was another man at his side, dressed similarly in clerical black. 'We are to have a guest preacher,' Miss Cardew remarked, lifting her lorgnette. 'That hat is quite becoming, Miss Bantry. A little flamboyant for church perhaps, but we must make allowances for your youth.'

It became impossible to linger any longer, and Virginia followed Mrs Kington inside. As the vicar stepped before the altar, her thoughts were far away, and she paid little attention to the service, until Reverend Porter beckoned to the black clad figure in a front pew.

There was a faint murmuring among the female members of the congregation; the vicar's guest had fair curly hair, smooth pale skin and open features. A week ago Virginia might have thought him good-looking, but today every new acquaintance must be compared to Simon Roper, and none could hope to outshine him.

As the vicar began his introduction the door opened at the back of the church, and Virginia spun round, but it was only Miss Cardew's brother, accompanied by a tall, slender gentleman with white hair, ducking into a pew at the back. Mrs Kington bent close to rebuke her charge, whispering in her ear. 'Be still, Virginia, please. This restlessness is so childish.'

Her cheeks colouring, Virginia returned her attention to the man who was about to ascend to the look pulpit. She caught the vicar's last words. '...Reverend Solcott.'

She could hardly believe her ears. This was their neighbour, tenant to Major Brand. The newcomer smiled down at the congregation, his gaze

64

sweeping across the rows of uplifted faces. Virginia had suspected this man, unseen, of threatening Simon's life. A flush rose to her cheeks. Nobody who looked like Reverend Solcott could be a rogue. He beamed upon the congregation, his face full of an almost childish pleasure.

'Today,' the man began, 'I shall speak to you of Christ's great mercy, and the lessons it behoves us to learn from his example.'

Virginia felt light-headed; it had always been ridiculous of course, to imagine the rogue who had treated Simon so badly could be a clergyman. The letter with its damning accusations seemed likely to burn its way out of the little bag; she couldn't pass the note to Simon now, even if he chose to appear after the service.

Practically squirming with embarrassment, Virginia found Reverend Solcott's pale eyes resting upon her. She forced herself to take a slow breath, as deep as her corset would allow. He had the face of an angel as he spoke of compassion and Christian charity; here was a man who would certainly be just as horrified as she, if he had been confronted with the evil deeds taking place in the cellar below Lucas Place a few nights before.

Thoroughly ashamed of herself, Virginia considered the items of evidence she had gathered. She had made much of the closed carriage coming and going from number four Lucas Place the previous afternoon, but the incident meant nothing. She had been stupid to think she could solve the puzzle simply by keeping watch on the street and gossiping with Cook.

Once the sermon was over, Virginia fidgeted,

desperate to hurry home and destroy the incriminating letter. She feared that Simon Roper might be waiting outside. Having no further notions of the Reverend Solcott's villainy, she felt she could no longer face Simon, even though neither man would know of her folly. Mrs Kington turned as if ready to reprimand her again, but was silenced when she saw her expression. 'Whatever is wrong, child?'

'I fear I have not quite thrown off the fever,' Virginia whispered. 'I am sorry, Mrs Kington, to be so ill-mannered, but I must go outside for some air.'

They made their way out as the congregation stood to sing a hymn. Insisting that she needed nothing but a few minutes of rest out of doors, Virginia sank on to a bench in the churchyard, her mind racing as fast as her pounding heart.

'Are you well enough to walk home?' Mrs Kington asked. 'If not we might secure a lift with Mr Cardew, I see he has his brougham waiting.'

Virginia shook her head; the thought of any company was unwelcome. 'I shall be well enough to walk in a few more minutes.'

'If you are still unwell tomorrow I shall call Dr Norris,' Mrs Kington said decidedly. 'It would not do for you to be indisposed when Sir Mortimer comes home. We must wait for some assistance, it would hardly do for you to suffer another collapse in the street.'

Virginia didn't argue. The service ended and the slow exodus began, with the vicar and his guest taking a leisurely farewell of the departing congregation. One or two people of their acquaintance came to speak to Mrs Kington and ask solicitously after Miss Bantry's health, and Virginia responded with a rueful smile, insisting that she was perfectly recovered.

'We must apologize to Reverend Porter and Reverend Solcott,' Mrs Kington said, as the crowd thinned. 'Then we must try to find somebody to take us home.'

Virginia nodded, though she had hardly heard her companion's words. The vicar was approaching, and behind him came their new neighbour.

'Mrs Kington,' Reverend Porter said, as he bustled up, 'what a very pleasant morning. And Miss Bantry. Are you feeling faint?'

'I am so sorry,' Virginia said, taking his outstretched hand, 'A slight indisposition. I should not have disrupted the service, but I had to have some air. Please forgive me.'

'There is nothing to forgive,' the vicar said. 'May I present Reverend Solcott, ladies? He professed himself eager to make your acquaintance. I understand he lives very close to you, but he hasn't yet had the pleasure of a formal introduction.'

The vicar's guest made his obeisance to Mrs Kington first, but his eyes dwelt far longer on Virginia. He took her hand, his gaze intense and his interest all too apparent. A little uncomfortable, she lowered her gaze from the light eyes that sought hers so keenly.

'Reverend Porter says you are our neighbour,' she said, addressing the hand which had captured her own, 'but I do not recall seeing you before.'

'I, on the other hand, have seen you several times, Miss Bantry. Unlike me, you are very much worthy of notice,' he added gallantly. 'I have taken Major Brand's house. Indeed, I have been there for nearly two months, and it was very remiss of me not to call upon you, particularly as Sir Mortimer Bantry is an old acquaintance.'

'He has been in South America, but we expect his return by the middle of this week,' Mrs Kington replied. 'Forgive me, I must make Miss Bantry's excuses, she has overtaxed herself. It is fortunate we have such a fine day, the walk will do her no harm.'

'Dare I say that Miss Bantry looks in the full bloom of health?' He continued to give her an appraising look, his lips curved in a delightful smile of approbation; had he not been a man of the cloth, Mrs Kington might have taken offence at such an open display of interest on his part. 'However, I am no judge of the humours of young ladies. If Miss Bantry is unwell perhaps even so short a walk would be unwise. My carriage is here, allow me to offer you both a ride, and give me the pleasure of your company a little longer.'

'That is very generous of you, sir,' Mrs Kington said.

'We were expecting Mr Cardew to take us,' Virginia put in untruthfully; she didn't care for the large and dyspeptic old man, who was inclined to ogle her and put his fleshy hand upon her knee at every opportunity, but she hardly felt equal to talking to a stranger, especially one who seemed set on making every sentence a compliment.

'But we are such near neighbours,' Solcott protested. 'Having neglected you up to now, I beg you will allow me to do you this small service.'

68

Before Virginia could think of a suitable reply, an interruption came from Mr Cardew himself. She could hear his laboured breathing, and smell his unpleasant breath, as he scurried up to join them, his large head looming over her shoulder.

'Mrs Kington, Miss Bantry. I thought I might have missed you. A friend of mine is eager to make your acquaintance. I didn't intend to arrive late. My health. As you know, I am a martyr to my digestion. Still, here we all are, eh? No harm done. Allow me to present Mr Roper, of the *City Examiner*.'

Virginia gasped. She had longed for him to be here, only to be profoundly grateful that he was not; now the worst had happened. He found her in conversation with a man who seemed intent on dallying with her in a most pointed manner, and she could see no polite way to refuse the offer of a lift in Reverend Solcott's carriage. With great reluctance she lifted her gaze to look at the tall figure emerging from behind Mr Cardew's bulk.

A pair of deep-blue eyes met hers. The sunny churchyard seemed to darken and tilt in a most unpleasant way. She was staring into Simon's eyes, and yet they looked at her from a face that was lined with age. The man had removed his hat, revealing a generous mop of white hair; he gazed down at her with a kindly expression, though he seemed a little puzzled by her lack of response to his greeting.

'Virginia!' Mrs Kington's voice was sharp.

'I'm so sorry,' she managed at last, 'I fear I am not so well after all. Mr Roper, Mr Cardew, forgive me.' She hardly knew what she was doing.

69

'Mrs Kington, I should like to go home. I believe we must accept Reverend Solcott's kind offer.'

'It will be my pleasure,' the clergyman said, tendering his arm.

Virginia leant on him as they bid their farewells. 'This is very kind of you, sir.'

'Nonsense, I am merely doing what any good neighbour would do. Don't rush now, only a few more steps,' he added solicitously.

At the carriage a large man climbed down from the box and opened the door as they approached. His forehead jutted low over small, red-rimmed eyes, and he had a bulbous nose that dominated his pock-marked face. Despite his being unprepossessing, and built upon a massive scale, like the giant she had half-seen in the cellar, Virginia was reassured; Mudd had worn rough working clothes and addressed his master with little respect, while Reverend Solcott's groom was immaculately dressed, and waited upon them in deferential silence.

Reverend Solcott handed the two ladies into his carriage, then called to his servant as he picked up the reins. 'You will drive slowly,' he ordered. 'The young lady is feeling unwell and doesn't wish to be jolted.'

'You are most considerate, sir,' Mrs Kington said, settling herself comfortably beside Virginia. 'Normally Mr Cardew would have taken us, but since he had his friend with him it may not have been convenient.'

'It is strange it has taken so long for us to meet, Mr Solcott,' Virginia said, eager not to allow Mr Roper's name to enter the conversation and seeking for a safer subject. 'I don't believe I've seen you at St Joseph's before.'

'*Mea culpa*,' he replied, giving her a grave smile. 'My duties have taken me elsewhere. But now I have met some of the congregation I feel this visit will not be my last.'

'You said you were acquainted with Sir Mortimer, my cousin. Where did you meet him?' Virginia asked, glancing out of the window. The groom had taken his master's words to heart, and the carriage was proceeding at a snail's pace.

'I encountered him in Liverpool, two years ago, and we had a most interesting conversation. I was delighted to find he was to be a near neighbour when I came to London. He spends so much of his time abroad, of course; he was bound for some remote and uncivilized place when we met. I recall telling him I did not envy him his journey.'

'You do not like to travel?'

'Only in civilized countries where I can be sure of a clean bed and decent food,' Solcott replied. 'My brother is the traveller in our family; he rarely remains in one place for more than a few months. When he comes to stay I never know how long to expect his company. I am happiest at home. I have observed that siblings are often very different. While my brother is very fond of riding on horseback, I much prefer the comfort of a carriage. Do you have brothers or sisters, Miss Bantry?'

'No, I'm afraid I have no family in the world apart from my cousin. Perhaps that is what makes him so dear to me.'

Solcott sighed heavily. 'You may be more fortunate than you realize. Close families can be a curse, as well as a blessing.'

Virginia tried to think of some polite way to encourage the clergyman to talk more about his troublesome brother, but the carriage was already making the turn into Lucas Place.

'Is there nothing more I can do?' Reverend Solcott queried, as he handed Virginia down. 'Perhaps you would allow me to send for your physician.'

'Oh no,' Virginia said quickly, before Mrs Kington could reply, 'we have trespassed upon your goodwill quite enough, sir. Thank you so very much.'

'Thank you indeed,' Mrs Kington echoed. 'I trust we shall see you again soon. Perhaps you would come and take tea with us tomorrow afternoon.'

Reverend Solcott shook his head with evident sorrow. 'That would have been delightful, but sadly I can't accept your invitation. I am due to visit a sick friend. It is a duty I am unable to postpone, and one that will take me away from Town for a week. I have several calls to make this afternoon, then I must catch the train early tomorrow morning.'

'I shall tell my cousin of your kindness,' Virginia said, 'and I am quite certain he will want to invite you to dinner, so we may all have the pleasure of your company.'

'I look forward to it. Good day, ladies.'

Virginia allowed Mrs Kington to hurry her inside, but resisted her companion's suggestion that Dr Norris should be called. 'I shall have a little

72

luncheon, and then I believe it would suit me well to sit quietly at my tapestry,' she said demurely.

Mrs Kington made no protest, although she watched with an eagle eye as Virginia ate.

'Before I go to my room for my rest,' she said, when the meal was over, 'I shall order camomile tea for us both. I suggest you lie down for a short while.'

Left alone, Virginia took the letter, now rather crumpled, from her mother's bag. Her cheeks flaming, she read what she had written, then tore the paper across and across, until it was no more than a heap of tiny scraps which she tossed into the fireplace. Sitting at her desk by the window, she took out paper and pen, but found herself unable to think of a thing to write. She wanted to see Simon Roper again, more than she had ever wanted anything in her life, but until that time came, it seemed there was nothing to be said.

The clock on the mantel chimed the quarter-hour, then the half. As Virginia's thoughts drifted, she became aware of movement outside the window. A carriage was passing by. Its blinds were down, which seemed strange on so fine a day. The horse slowed and swung wide as the vehicle neared the end of the street; either it was entering Newscombe Street, or the rear entrance of the last two houses in Lucas Place.

As the carriage turned she saw the blind twitch. A shape, pale against the dark fabric, appeared for the briefest moment. It was a hand, so small that it could only belong to a child, but before she had time to register exactly what she had seen, the pale shape was engulfed in a larger fist and snatched away. The blind fell back into place.

'Virginia? What will people think, seeing you practically hanging from the window! Show a little decorum, I beg you.' Mrs Kington's unwelcome remonstrance brought Virginia spinning round. By the time she glanced out of the window again the carriage had gone.

'It is almost time for evensong. I had hoped to find you fully recovered.' Mrs Kington's tone carried a reproach.

'I am sorry.' Virginia expressed a regret she didn't feel. 'I hope you will not mind if I stay at home. I am still rather distracted, and I don't wish to be an inconvenience to you.'

'Caring for you is my duty. Perhaps I should stay.'

'I assure you it isn't necessary.' Virginia attempted a smile. 'Given solitude I hope I shall rid myself of this bad humour. You are very patient, but I don't like to try you too far.'

Her companion gave her a long and searching look, as if trying to measure the sincerity of this double-edged remark. 'There are times when you try me, to be sure,' she said eventually, 'but I have no wish to see you either unwell or unhappy. I shall go to evensong, and leave orders that you are not to be disturbed.'

'I shall easily find occupations suitable for a Sunday afternoon,' Virginia said, though she doubted Mrs Kington would have agreed with this judgement, had she been aware of her intentions.

Chapter Seven

A little later Virginia peeped out of the window to watch her companion walk away across Lucas Place. The idea of visiting the cellar again had been with her ever since she watched the closed carriage go by. Having met Reverend Solcott she had no further suspicions of him; before she could feel comfortable about meeting the man again, she would establish his innocence by identifying the house where Simon Roper had been held prisoner.

As for the carriage, there was no doubt in her mind. The blinds were drawn down despite the fine weather, and a child's hand was snatched from the blind by that of a large man; she had witnessed another *piece of merchandise* being delivered to its cruel fate.

The lives of poor children were often short and brutal, maybe beyond Virginia's capacity to imagine, despite the experience she had gained on her travels. She saw ragged scraps of humanity begging on the streets, and thought nothing of it, either in the heat of an African bazaar or the chill damp of a London street corner. If the question was raised in polite company, it would be pointed out that no amount of charity could change the way of the world. Virginia couldn't have explained why the fate of these girls was so different; it was not only that she wished to make herself useful to

Simon Roper. Perhaps it was the memory of that sweltering day in the bazaar. The eyes of that small child, making her desperate bid for freedom, would never stop haunting her. And now there was a smooth, cultured voice to disturb her peace, alleging that human life had no value, a bagatelle to be snuffed out with barely a thought, and with no expectation of punishment. She shuddered, thinking of the lifted flagstone in the floor, and the way the filthy water had greedily gobbled up the chair when they had tipped it into the abyss.

For one brief second Virginia almost wished she hadn't ventured into the cellar, but then she would never have met Simon, and by now he would probably be dead. Nevertheless, she would rather not have heard the words that had been drawn so reluctantly from his lips when she taunted him. He had tried to be chivalrous, and she had accused him of cowardice.

'They kidnap young children and sell them.' He had forced her to think the unthinkable, and she could not undo what was done, so now she must move and do what she could to fight this evil trade. There were things to be learned from the cellar. Those men came from close by, but the mews was a busy place; it would be hard to conceal the arrival and departure of kidnapped children at a place where trade started early in the morning and went on well into the night. She was sure the cellar must belong to one of the nearby houses, unless, she thought suddenly, unless the children never stayed long, but were simply transferred from one carriage to another, and what Simon Roper had stumbled upon was no more than a staging post.

With Mrs Kington and most of the servants out of the way, Virginia would have an hour to herself, which should be time enough. Running swiftly downstairs with an ungainly haste which would have brought a horrified admonition from Mrs Kington, Virginia fetched an oil lamp from the hall; it should give a better light than Willshire's ancient lantern. As she pushed the cellar key into the lock, a slight sound from beyond the green baize door caught her attention; somebody was washing the floor. The kitchen door opened slowly, just a crack, and she could see a bright eye peering at her. It was Emily.

Smiling, Virginia pressed a finger to her lips. The door slid shut, and the sound of scrubbing resumed with a new vigour. Stepping through the cellar door, Virginia descended from the sunlit hall. She left the door wide open behind her this time, with the key in the lock; it would be heartening to know that a quick exit awaited her.

Taking the spool of thread once more in her hand, Virginia set out to retrace the route of her previous visit, and found the way to Miss Forswick's cellar without any difficulty. She felt sure there should be a direct connection to the cellar below number three; the winding route she had taken to the place of Simon's imprisonment seemed a long way round, if that was indeed where it lay. She couldn't recall ever seeing Mr Parkin; perhaps his seclusion was a cover for a criminal enterprise, unless the smooth-voiced man was his son, returned to his old home in secret. Since the old man never left his rooms, he might be making use of the cellars without the elderly invalid's knowledge.

Virginia explored several dead ends, but always returned to the entrance to Miss Forswick's cellar. She decided to make one more attempt, until a familiar sound brought her to a halt. Somebody in her cousin's house had closed the cellar door. Quite clearly, echoing through the silence, she heard the key turn in the lock.

'You say she was ill?' Simon Roper paced the room in agitation. 'Some sort of nervous indisposition, do you think? She acted with such courage, but perhaps the events of the other night were too much for her. If only you had allowed me to go with you.'

'That would have been unwise.' Jocelyn Roper watched his nephew with some concern. 'We still don't know the name of the man responsible for taking you captive, and you admit you might not recognize him, even if you come face to face. While these people assume that you are dead, it makes sense for you to stay well away from that neighbourhood. If this rogue masquerades as a gentleman, he might well have been in the congregation this morning. Besides, you must give yourself time to recover; you are supposed to be resting.'

This was dismissed with a wave of Simon's good hand. 'My bones will heal in their own time, and the headaches have almost gone. A little exercise is a good thing when one is convalescing, why shouldn't I take a stroll as far as St Joseph's for evensong?'

'That's out of the question.' Jocelyn rose to his feet in evident agitation. 'You are to take no more

78

risks. If you truly feel recovered and wish to make yourself useful, I have a quantity of notes sent to me by a patron of the Magdalene Home for Fallen Women. This information needs collating and evaluating before I write my next editorial.'

Simon wasn't listening. 'You were introduced to several of the congregation, so even if Miss Bantry doesn't attend we may still get news of her.'

His uncle sighed. 'Since you are so persistent, I have another suggestion. Mr Cardew was kind enough to ask me to supper, and he extended the invitation to include you. His sister is a particular friend of Miss Bantry's companion, so she could safely be asked for a report on the young lady's health. I suppose you are well enough to come, but you must not exert yourself. We shall hire a cab, and make our excuses no later than ten o'clock.'

'Thank you, sir.' Jocelyn's expression brightened. 'And meanwhile I'll willingly study those notes, and see if there's anything to be made of them.'

'These are mostly the work of a Mrs Marchant.' Jocelyn Roper picked up a sheaf of papers from his desk. 'The Magdalene Home deals primarily with the reform of street women wishing to mend their ways, so not much will be relevant. The trade in the very young tends to be both more secretive, and more selective. There must be bawdy houses specializing in that perversion, but they are well hidden. Try to focus on anything referring to children, particularly any who were stolen, or hired as servants. They could come from within the city's poorest areas, but also from country districts many miles from London.'

'If a child is bought from its parents, does

anybody have the right to interfere?' Simon asked. 'The poor do not see things as we do. To many of them a child is no more than a burden, another mouth to feed. Are you sure we are right to judge them by our standards?'

'I don't judge them, as you put it, by our standards or any other, but to introduce a child to the sexual act at the tender age of six or seven is a most shameful crime. Imagine how it might scar a young mind, as well as an immature body. There have been cases where the parents have been assured that the girl is to be adopted by some wealthy woman who has no child of her own. They let their daughter go, believing it is in her best interests. The law is slow to respond, it is time children were given protection from these people.'

'I suspect that whether your campaign is successful or not, there will still be men and women willing to sell their child for a few shillings,' Simon said.

Jocelyn sighed. 'I don't doubt it. The fact that an evil exists, and has always existed, doesn't make it any less wrong. This trade had increased recently, even the police admit it, although they profess themselves helpless to act. Of course, some officers are lazy or dishonest, others are uncaring, but there are good men in the force. I have met with one detective, a man I have reason to trust, who claims that there is a criminal mastermind behind this particular network of procurers, a figure of considerable social standing.'

'Does this villain have a name?'

'Inspector Laker says he has yet to uncover it, but he would be interested in hearing of any developments which may assist his enquiries.'

'He wants us to do his work for him,' Simon said, his mouth quirking down.

'No; he's being cautious. Possibly an influential person has attempted to warn him off, informing him that pursuing this particular rogue could prove damaging to his future in the police detective division,' Jocelyn said. 'I have some sympathy for him.'

'I have heard that most policemen turn a blind eye to prostitution, while the worst of them take their share from street women, in return for allowing them to ply their trade.'

'That goes on, certainly,' Jocelyn conceded, 'and the law as it stands condones such behaviour, perhaps even encourages it. But we are concerned with children. I believe if the facts about these infants were known, we would have the co-operation of all honest officers.'

'Our role must be to inform men of influence,' Simon mused. 'There would be uproar if we succeeded in taking a case to court; nobody could claim that we were only interested in selling the *Examiner* if we succeeded in putting this so-called mastermind in the dock!'

'That would require evidence. The word of those who suffer at the hands of these men won't bear much weight, since the victims are not only young but female. However, through the good offices of the Magdalene Home, one or two of these children have been rescued and rehabilitated. Unfortunately Mrs Marchant is reluctant to allow us to interview any of her charges.'

Jocelyn tapped a finger on the papers before

81

putting them down in front of Simon. 'You must look for some pattern, a common factor that will give us an understanding of how this trade operates. We must act with circumspection, and not make a move until we are sure of our ground, for the sake of Mrs Marchant and her friends.'

'The people of London should know what is going on,' Simon protested.

Jocelyn Roper shook his head. 'I ask you to recall your own encounter with them. These are ruthless people.' He was still reluctant to tell his nephew about his meeting with the government minister; Mrs Marchant might be under similar pressure. He consulted his watch. 'I shall leave you to your work now. The cab will be ordered for seven.'

Virginia held her breath, watching as the flame in the lamp wavered; she was terrified that it would go out. How could she have forgotten to bring the matchbox and candles. Hissing slightly, the feeble blue flame brought a ghastly hue to all it touched. She tried to turn up the wick, but it seemed to be stuck. If Willshire had returned and locked the door, she might be trapped for hours before anyone thought to look for her in the cellar.

She thrust her knuckles into her mouth to keep herself from crying out. Primeval fears assailed her; the nameless demons that dwelt in the dark recesses of the earth were suddenly very real, more terrible than the underground maze, or the noisome drop into filthy swirling waters, and more threatening than merciless men who spoke of murder.

A sibilant murmur came softly to her ears. Could it be the lost boy? It sounded as if the worn stones beneath her feet had found a voice.

'Are you there?'

The whisper echoed from the walls and filled the vaulted chambers, coming from every direction and yet none. Mindful of the lost boy, Virginia forgot that she didn't believe in ghosts, and dug her fingernails into her palms in an effort to keep herself from screaming.

'Miss? Are you there?'

Not a ghost, but a child. It was a voice she knew.

'Emily?' Virginia's voice was a little shrill; she was only a heartbeat away from collapse. Shock and relief came together to set her whole body trembling. She let out a long sighing breath, her body sagging against the rough stone at her back. The little maid came running towards her, a stub of candle guttering in her hand.

'Whatever are you doing down here?' Virginia demanded. 'Who locked the door?'

'Hush,' the girl said urgently. She handed Virginia the key to the cellar. 'I'm sorry, miss, but I didn't know what else to do when Mr Willshire came back. He didn't go to church at all. I heard him telling Cook he had too much to do, and that he was going to check on the wine, because Sir Mortimer had given him special instructions about the cellar. When he went to fetch his keys from the pantry, there wasn't time to come and warn you, and I didn't think you'd want Mr Willshire to know you were down here. Was I wrong, miss?' Even as Emily finished speaking, they heard the scrape of a key in the lock.

'Quickly!' Virginia dragged the girl through the nearest arch, shielding the feebly flickering lamp and gesturing to the girl to blow out the candle.

Small sounds reached them where they crouched in the dark. Having recovered from her fright, and with the cellar key safely in her pocket, Virginia had to bite down the temptation to laugh. The situation was ridiculous; she was hiding from her cousin's butler, crouching in the shadowy basement like a fugitive, and with a kitchen maid at her side. No doubt Willshire would have been displeased to find her there, but she could have found a way to deal with him. Poor Emily. It had been very brave of her to come, perhaps imagining that Virginia had as much to fear from the butler as she did.

Willshire moved about among the wine racks, but then they heard the door of the wine cellar slam shut. To Virginia's consternation, the man's footsteps, instead of receding up the steps to the house, were getting louder. The light grew brighter, he was coming their way. Had he seen something to make him suspect he wasn't alone?

Pushing Emily further into the darkness, Virginia hid the lamp with her skirt, feeling its heat against her. It was too late to brazen things out; she might escape with no more than a loss of dignity, but she would be powerless to protect the girl.

The light from Willshire's lantern was approaching the place where they were hidden. If the butler turned his head he must surely see them. Virginia could feel the child shaking, and put a warning hand on her shoulder. The man passed by, his boots ringing on the flags. He seemed to know his way, for he walked briskly, looking neither to left nor right.

As soon as he was gone Emily began to creep back towards the wine cellar, but Virginia stopped her. 'Wait,' she whispered. She could scarcely believe what she was seeing; was her cousin's dignified butler involved in the sordid business of kidnapping and murder?

Virginia hesitated, trying to make some sense of her whirling thoughts. In a few more moments the light from Willshire's lamp would vanish, and the chance would be gone. It had always been her intention to find a way out of the labyrinth; this was too good an opportunity to miss. A dull glow on the wall showed her where Willshire had turned from the main passageway. Taking hold of the maid's trembling hand Virginia pulled her into motion. 'Come along,' she said quietly, 'let's find out where he's going.'

Chapter Eight

They had to hurry. The light from Willshire's lantern was no more than a faint glow reflecting upon a dark wall as they approached the turn he had taken. Here Virginia gave Emily the lamp. 'Keep a little behind me,' she said, 'and try not to let the light show.' It looked as if the man was too intent upon his own business to notice them, but she didn't want to be seen. Almost running, Virginia unravelled the thread as they took several more turns through chambers and passages that were completely unfamiliar to her. She hesitated at the entrance to a narrow tunnel where the roof was so low that she had to bend her head to avoid hitting it; the walls and floor here were of rough hewn rock, unlike any she had seen so far. There were no side passages; if Willshire looked back he must see them. She caught a glimpse of him, far ahead. The man was bent almost double, but hadn't slackened his pace.

'Please, miss,' Emily breathed, 'I dassen't go on. I'll be in such trouble.'

'No, you won't, I'll see nobody blames you for coming with me,' Virginia said. 'There's nothing to worry about, he's turned another corner, so he can't see us. Come on, we don't want to lose him.' A small sound from Emily suggested that the maid didn't agree, but the child kept her place, treading as lightly as a ghost over the uneven ground.

Beneath her fingers Virginia could feel that the spool of thread was almost empty; she muttered a silent prayer that it would not run out, for she was not so foolhardy as to go on without it. Abruptly the low ceiling was gone. Virginia could stand upright again and they were in a straight brick-lined tunnel.

With a hiss of warning Virginia snatched the lamp and thrust it against the wall, draping her skirts to hide its feeble flame. Far ahead a different sort of light shone, startlingly bright. Its rays illuminated the dusty stone floor and almost reached their feet, but then as quickly as it had appeared it was cut off, and all was dark.

'That was daylight,' Virginia said wonderingly. 'He's gone.'

'Mr Willshire might not be long, miss,' Emily said, wringing her hands anxiously. 'Please, let's go back.'

Virginia bit her lip, tempted to take a closer look, but the child was right; she didn't want to be found here. She didn't really believe that Willshire's dash through the tunnels had any connection with Mudd, or the wicked trade he and his master were involved in, but it would be stupid to take chances. She stepped back from the lamp and wrestled with it, getting a bright flame this time. 'We'll go back,' she said. 'But we'll mark the way. He'd see the thread, and we'd never remember all those twists and turns.' Pulling out a hairpin, she bent to scratch a tiny arrow on the stone wall, close to the floor where it wouldn't be noticed.

'Please, miss, quickly!' Emily was almost hopping on the spot in her eagerness to be gone. Glancing back now and then, grateful to see no sign of Wilshire's return, they retraced their steps, the maid leading the way, and Virginia marking their passage. She hadn't identified which house stood above the chamber where she'd found Simon, but she daren't stay any longer, because Mrs Kington would be back soon. She wouldn't abandon the child she had seen in the carriage, but her next visit must be at night.

'Miss?' Emily's voice recalled Virginia to the present. The maid stood by the opening that gave on to Miss Forswick's cellar. From here Virginia was confident of her way; there was no need for any further arrows. She tucked the bent hairpin back into place.

'Don't worry, I'll make sure Cook doesn't scold you,' Virginia said.

'Thank you, miss.' Looking relieved the maid almost skipped the rest of the way, past the wine cellar and up the steps. 'Where do you think Mr Willshire went, miss?'

'I don't know, but I think we know what happened to that missing kitchen boy.'

'What, the one who stole the duck?' Emily's mouth dropped open. 'Really, miss?'

Virginia laughed as she closed the door behind them and locked it. 'Is that what he did? I don't believe my cousin ever told me that part of the story.'

'So Cook said. But he got his comeuppance; he got lost and starved to death.'

'That's just a fairy-tale,' Virginia said, laughing again. 'Believe me, he'll be a grown man by now. That kitchen boy must have known the way through the tunnels just like Willshire, and he ran away rather than face a beating. He's probably been living off his wits ever since, and he'll have stolen a lot more than a duck, unless he turned over a new leaf.'

Virginia put the lamp away, and hid the spool of thread in the armoire by the front parlour window, while Emily stood uneasily in the hall. 'There, nobody will know what we have been doing,' Virginia said. 'I'll tell Cook that you were helping me so she won't scold.'

'No, miss. Wait!' Emily darted forwards and began brushing her hands down Virginia's clothes. 'You're all dusty. And look, the lantern has scorched your skirt.'

The brown streak couldn't be missed on the blue poplin. Virginia sighed; she would be the one being scolded. 'Mrs Kington will enjoy reading me a lecture about carelessness.'

Cook made no difficulty about Emily's absence, not questioning Virginia's story about enlisting her help with sorting tapestry wools. 'I've not needed her,' she said, as the girl scurried back to her work. 'But you'd best not let Mr Willshire catch you giving the child such treats. He seemed a little short when he came home.'

'Did he?' Virginia was instantly interested. 'Do you think something is wrong?'

'He didn't say; he went down to the cellar with hardly a word. I daresay it will be something to do with the wine Sir Mortimer ordered, ready for his homecoming.'

'But he wouldn't have heard about that on a Sunday, would he?'

Cook shrugged. 'I'm sure I wouldn't know.'

Virginia glanced at the kitchen clock; her companion would be back from evensong very soon. Hurrying to the baize door, she was almost bowled over when Wilshire came rushing through. An angry complaint had half formed in his throat before he realized who was blocking his way; red-faced, looking as though he was barely in control of himself, the butler barked an apology. He held the door open for Virginia to leave, letting it close so quickly that she felt it brush her heels as she passed through.

As she walked away Virginia thought she heard raised voices; although she was intrigued, good manners forbade her to linger and eavesdrop at the door. She couldn't help but wonder at Willshire's strange behaviour though; she could never recall seeing him less than calm and dignified in all her years at Lucas Place. Slowly mounting the stairs, the image of the man's angry face seemed to go before her, and with the vision came a startling revelation; there had been another emotion in Willshire's eyes. The butler was afraid.

By the time Mrs Kington returned, some ten minutes later, Virginia was settled at her tapestry frame. She greeted her companion cheerfully, showing off her handiwork. 'I should have no trouble completing it for my cousin's home-coming,' she said.

'Certainly you have shown some application. And I am pleased to see your colour has returned to normal.' Mrs Kington hesitated, as if about to add something.

'Is there anything wrong?' Virginia asked.

'Not wrong, but I face a dilemma. We have had an invitation, but I am not sure it would be wise to accept. Miss Cardew and her brother asked if you are sufficiently recovered to take supper with them. They are to have two other guests: Mr Roper, the gentleman who was introduced to us so briefly this morning, and the young man whom you rescued from the street the other morning, who is evidently his nephew.'

'Roper! Of course, I recall hearing the name now, though everything happened so very quickly and in such confusion,' Virginia said, all innocence. 'Well, the older gentleman dresses a great deal better than the younger.'

Mrs Kington gave her a sharp look. 'I have been assured that as far as our unexpected guest is concerned, appearances the other morning were deceptive, and that Mr Simon Roper is not only respectable, but well connected.' She gave an expressive sniff. 'I suppose an introduction at the Cardews' would allow us to form our own judgement.'

'I should like to go,' Virginia said, keeping her eyes lowered to her work and doing her best to appear calm; Mrs Kington much preferred Miss Cardew's company to hers, but she took her duties seriously; she wouldn't take Virginia out if she feared for her health. 'I would like to apologize to Mr Roper for my behaviour this morning.'

'Mr Cardew is willing to send his carriage,' Mrs Kington said, obviously vacillating, 'and we need not stay late.'

'It would be pleasant to be able to tell my cousin that we have made a new acquaintance,' Virginia put in, still busy with her needle. 'Our lives here provide very little of interest, compared with all the traveller's tales he will have to relate.'

Mrs Kington's expression softened, by the smallest degree. 'Very well, I shall send a message. Do not tire your eyes by working too long, it will spoil your looks.' She left, and Virginia was free to revel in the knowledge that she was to see Simon that very evening.

After wasting several minutes on romantic speculation, her thoughts turned to practical matters. There were things she wanted to convey to the Ropers, which couldn't be spoken of in company, such as Willshire's obvious familiarity with the labyrinth beyond the wine cellar. Sitting at her desk, she began with an account of the tall, soldierly man who had appeared so frequently in Lucas Place over the last few days; she hesitated over the account of the closed carriage, flushing as she recalled her embarrassment when she met Reverend Solcott and determined to write nothing which might cast doubt on an innocent man. After great deliberation she described exactly what she had seen; she then wrote briefly about her meeting with her neighbour, with a summary of his character, as far as it could be judged on one brief encounter. She would leave Simon to come to his own conclusions.

Virginia sighed. Above all things, she wanted to talk to Simon. He hadn't come to church, but if she named another time and place where they might meet, apparently by accident, would he choose to come? There was only one way to find out. She had arranged to meet Mrs Yelding the following afternoon, and join her in a walk through the park. The elderly widow had a surprisingly relaxed attitude to propriety, but was eminently respectable, not to mention being trusted by Mrs Kington. Dipping her pen into the ink, Virginia added a postscript, signing it with her initials. After that she spent a pleasurable half-hour deciding what she should wear for the evening, finally choosing a costume with rather military lines. It showed off her small waist, and it had large pockets, ideal for concealing a letter.

Simon moved his chair to the window where the light was better, but the headache he'd suffered ever since his encounter with Mudd was still dogging him. He had been struggling with the papers for over an hour; they were written in a small, cramped hand, and did nothing to help the pain behind his eyes.

Mrs Marchant didn't have a well-organized system when it came to keeping records of her work. In many cases the age of the entrant into the Magdalene Home wasn't mentioned, and very few of the reformed prostitutes had given information about their original slide into a life of degradation. Those who did were eager to place the blame on anyone but themselves, saying they had been forced or tricked into the trade when too young to know better, but it was hard to come to the truth of the matter.

Despite this, Simon concluded that his uncle's observation was correct; the market for small children, certainly where it was run for men of means, was conducted with great discretion. There were oblique references made to girls brought to the notice of Mrs Marchant and her fellow philanthropists by other women, either prostitutes or procurers themselves. Presumably these females had a little humanity left in them, and felt moved to try to protect these lost innocents from their own fate.

Simon had found one case of great interest, although it didn't directly involve the Magdalene Home. The incident had been brought to Mrs Marchant's notice by a magistrate, a friend of her husband, and she had thought it important enough to record.

An eight-year-old girl had been snatched while

she was working with several other children, stone picking for a local landowner. A closed carriage had stopped on a nearby road, and a lady had got out, approaching the child and offering her a ride, and possibly a meal, though the other children weren't too clear on this point. Her brother, a bright child a year younger than his sister, tried to dissuade her from accepting, but the girl didn't listen, climbing into the carriage and being whisked away.

It wasn't until evening, when the child was still missing, that the alarm was raised. The child was unusual – and fortunate – in having a father who was well thought of, despite his poverty. When he appealed for help to the squire, the same man who had employed the child, that gentleman agreed to contact the local magistrate. He then sent a clerk along the London road to enquire after the carriage. Evidently feeling responsible for the fate of an employee, albeit a small and insignificant one, the landowner also had the news cried in the two closest towns the next morning, appealing for the return of the girl, with the offer of a reward.

It seemed likely the kidnappers were dismayed by this interest on the girl's behalf, for within twelve hours she was brought back, by a man claiming to have found her abandoned by the road, ten miles from home. There were no further details; no mention was made of the child's own recollection of her abduction, nor was her brother's account given. The name of the man who was rewarded for returning the child wasn't noted; it seemed likely that the villains had claimed the money themselves.

Simon rose to pour himself a drink, rubbing his forehead. His mind was as tired as his eyes. Somewhere in the house a door slammed. He looked up at the clock; it was almost time to leave. Jocelyn Roper was in the hall when his nephew came downstairs, having sent his manservant to summon a cab. 'Are you sure you wish to come?' the older man asked. 'You look tired.'

'A little company is exactly what I need,' Simon replied lightly. Once they were seated in the cab he broached the subject uppermost in his mind. 'Sir, I should like your permission to approach Mrs Marchant.'

'You think you can persuade her to let you interview her charges where I have failed?'

Simon grinned. 'I'm a victim of these rogues, sir, she may take pity on me.'

'Even with your hand in a sling, I doubt if she will be softened by your youth or your looks,' Jocelyn replied drily, 'but I have an appointment to see her tomorrow morning at ten. I see no reason why you shouldn't accompany me.'

'Such a shame Miss Bantry is indisposed,' Mr Cardew said, giving Jocelyn Roper a ponderous wink as he welcomed his two visitors, 'I sent an invitation, but I rather gathered from Mrs Kington that the young lady will probably stay home this evening. It's a pity. We old men don't often get to enjoy the company of a pretty girl, and such a spirited one too.'

His sister looked down her long nose at him, her narrow features expressing her disapproval of his comment, or maybe the girl who formed the subject of it. 'If by spirited you mean she is inclined to flout the proprieties, then I hardly think that is a quality to be applauded. Mr Roper will be able to form his own conclusions. Did I not tell you I received a message, Howard? The young lady has recovered; she and Mrs Kington'll be here shortly.'

'I'm glad to hear it,' Jocelyn replied, giving his nephew a warning glance; the young man's face was suddenly animated, his cheeks flushing and his eyes bright. 'It is strange I never met my old friend's ward before. I believe Sir Mortimer is expected very soon?'

'This week. It's a shame Major Brand is no longer in residence in Lucas Place; he would have given a party to celebrate the wanderer's home-coming,' Cardew said. 'I didn't think much of his latest tenant this morning. I like a preacher with a bit of fire in his belly, this namby-pamby milk and water stuff makes for a poor sermon.'

'I don't believe I'm acquainted with Major Brand,' Jocelyn Roper remarked.

'He owns number four, Lucas Place. But he's not been there for the last two years.'

'It was a great tragedy,' Miss Cardew said. 'His wife died suddenly, and the poor man was quite inconsolable. He put his children into school and went rushing off to South Africa. The house has been let to several tenants since then. Personally I consider Reverend Solcott a worthy addition to our society. I enjoyed his address; at least it was original. Reverend Porter becomes increasingly lazy; it is bad enough that he takes all his sermons from books, but I do wish he wouldn't repeat them with such frequency.'

'Would number four be at the end of Lucas Place,' Simon asked, 'three doors from Sir Mortimer's house?'

'Yes, that's right,' Miss Cardew replied. 'I was shocked to hear that you were set upon in such a neighbourhood. There are tradesmen living in Newscombe Street, and, of course, there is the mews, but despite that the area is respectable.'

'No telling what rogues will get up to at night,' Mr Cardew put in. 'but I doubt it's anything to worry about. As for Solcott, what I think of him won't matter to the young ladies hereabouts. They'll be pleased with this newcomer to our society. He whisked our Miss Bantry away from under my very nose this morning, before we'd had time to exchange more than a word or two. I was hoping to be allowed to escort her home myself, but I suppose you can't blame the child for preferring the company of an eligible young clergyman.'

'We know nothing about the man, you can't assume his eligibility,' his sister said.

'I am assured that he is single, like Miss Bantry. She'd be quite a catch.' Cardew gave Simon a nudge, a smile that was more like a leer upon his face. 'You can't tell me you didn't notice that when you met her, eh?'

'Really, Howard, you forget yourself,' his sister snapped. There was a knock at the door, and they heard footsteps as a servant went to answer the summons. 'I trust this will be the rest of our party.'

Simon thrust his injured hand into the front of his waistcoat; the beat of his heart was suddenly more urgent, thudding against the bruises that circled his wrist.

Chapter Nine

Virginia was careful to hide her excitement; Mrs Kington might order the carriage to turn round if she showed signs of feverishness. As they were carried through the streets she had kept her thoughts firmly focused on her companion, who regaled her with an account of Miss Cardew's latest dispute with her dressmaker.

With a feeling of unreality, Virginia stepped into the drawing room of Mr Cardew's house, catching sight of her reflection in a mirror. Her colour was all Mrs Kington could wish; her cheeks were becomingly pale and she looked cool and calm, despite her racing pulse. Being introduced again to Jocelyn Roper, Virginia apologized for her conduct that morning, careful not to let her gaze drift to the young man who stood so attentively at his uncle's shoulder. The elder Mr Roper waved away her apology, and having been assured that she was quite recovered, he beckoned his nephew forward.

'Mrs Kington, Miss Bantry, permit me to introduce my brother's son, Simon. I understand he owes you a considerable debt. It was very kind of you both to take pity on a stranger in need of succour.' Virginia met the deep-blue eyes and caught the ghost of a twinkle in them, as Simon was making an impeccable bow over Mrs Kington's hand.

'A Christian could do no less,' Mrs Kington replied.

'You were both so very kind,' Simon said, risking a glance in Virginia's direction.

'How strange,' Virginia cried. 'From your speech, now and at our door, you would be judged a gentleman, Mr Roper, but you didn't look like one the other morning.'

He turned to her, and once again she felt that surge of warmth, exciting and yet rather alarming. His eyes were alight with mischief. 'You saw me at a disadvantage,' he said. 'I dressed as a workman to gather information for a piece I wished to write for the *Examiner*. It was a silly prank, and now I doubt I shall ever persuade you to take me seriously.'

'Is he ever serious?' Virginia asked, turning to the older man.

'He can be. At times he addresses himself to our business with great aptitude and considerable dedication.'

'A glowing testimonial,' Miss Cardew said. 'Perhaps you are prejudiced, being the young man's uncle as well as his employer. Come, let us go in for supper. Mr Roper, would you give Miss Bantry your arm, in case she feels a return of this morning's weakness?'

Virginia felt a flush rise to her cheeks at his touch. The slight tremble in his fingers told her he was similarly ill at ease, and that steadied her. A radiant smile lit her face. 'You weren't at St Joseph's with your uncle this morning,' she said lightly.

'Business kept me occupied elsewhere,' he

replied, 'but I trust you won't consider me a heathen. I shall hope to prove it by attending every service next Sunday.'

'Sir Mortimer Bantry will be home by then,' Mrs Kington put in, turning back to look at them, her voice a little sharp as if she had sensed something deeper than their exchange of words suggested. 'He doesn't always attend St Joseph's; naturally Miss Bantry and I shall accompany him if he chooses to worship elsewhere.'

Seemingly unabashed Simon smiled at her, his expression suitably meek. 'Of course. I have no wish to presume, although I hope for the honour of meeting Sir Mortimer when he renews his acquaintance with my uncle.'

Mrs Kington seemed mollified, perhaps even impressed with his manners; it was a good start. Virginia found herself seated between Mr Cardew and the elder Mr Roper. This meant that Simon was seated across the table from her, and it was hard to avoid meeting his eyes.

'How is your hand, Mr Roper?' Miss Cardew asked. 'Not badly injured I trust?'

'No,' Simon replied, 'an inconvenience more than anything.'

'It was unwise to go out in disguise at night,' Jocelyn Roper declared, 'but we must put that particular misadventure down to my nephew's youth and inexperience.'

Virginia felt anger rise in her like a tide. It seemed almost as if he believed Simon had been hurt through his own carelessness; it was all she could do not to make an angry retort, but Simon's voice stopped her.

'I really should have known better than to take such a risk,' he acknowledged, 'there is no excuse for carelessness. What happened to my hand was entirely my own fault, and it could easily have led to other people being hurt, had anyone tried to intervene.' Although he didn't look at Virginia she knew the remark was intended for her. 'That would have been unforgivable, and I shall certainly take a great deal more care in future.'

The conversation turned to other matters, and Virginia let the talk flow around her, putting in a word or two when necessary; as the youngest and least at the table, she wasn't required to take much part. She stole occasional glances at Simon, exerting all his charm upon Mrs Kington and Miss Cardew, her thoughts running wild. An undeniable attraction existed between herself and Simon Roper; she knew he felt it as she did, it was there in the way he looked at her, and the bright rush of colour to his cheeks whenever their eyes met.

Sometimes when she moved Virginia was conscious of the letter in her pocket; she must find a way to deliver it, but how much better it would be if she could talk to him! She wanted to know if he had learned any more about Mudd and his smooth-voiced master.

All too soon, the meal was over. Because of Virginia's supposedly fragile health, Mrs Kington had made it plain on their arrival that they would not stay long; at any moment she might pass a hint to Mr Cardew about the carriage, and although Virginia had managed to remove the letter from her pocket and conceal it beneath her thigh, she could see no way to pass it to Simon without being detected. In desperation she turned to Jocelyn Roper. 'Does your company print anything apart from the *City Examiner?*' she asked. 'I have often thought my cousin's adventures would make an exciting book.'

'I have said as much to him many times,' Mr Roper said, 'and begged him to allow me to be the one to publish his memoirs, but I'm afraid my appeals have fallen on deaf ears. Sir Mortimer has always said he is too busy living his life to sit down and write about it. Perhaps in another twenty years he will slow down. After all, he is still quite a young man.'

'He was only twenty-five when he took over guardianship of his cousin,' Mrs Kington put in, her disapproval of his youth quite evident.

'But he has taken very good care of me,' Virginia said. 'I have no complaint, except that I would prefer to join him in his travels; I considered myself very fortunate that he chose not to return directly from India. We had such exciting times. I wrote an account of our journey across Africa,' she added, leaning towards Jocelyn Roper as if to emphasize what she was saying. 'Writing is such a pleasure, I find, as well as a means of communication.' She pushed the letter on to the seat of his chair, and was relieved to see his fingers close about the paper and slip it into his own pocket.

'I agree there is a great satisfaction to be gained from writing,' Jocelyn said, 'even though I have earned my living from the printed word for many years, I still enjoy sitting down with a fresh sheet of paper before me.'

'I've been following this brouhaha of yours over

the last week or two, Roper,' Mr Cardew declared, 'I must say it makes shocking reading. Frightfully young, some of these girls, eh? Are you sure it's true? Where do you get your information?'

'As I have mentioned in my most recent article, there are people who perform great works of charity amongst the most needy and unfortunate of the city's poor. I know you are acquainted with Mrs Marchant.'

'Oh, Lord, yes,' Cardew nodded. 'Her family has plenty of money, but she spends most of it on good causes, and then comes round badgering her neighbours for subscriptions. All very admirable I suppose, but it's a wonder her husband puts up with it. What kind of wife spends her time mixing with a lot of–' He broke off as his sister gave a meaningful cough.

'This is hardly a suitable subject for discussion, Howard,' Miss Cardew said reprovingly, glancing at Virginia.

Virginia lowered her eyes; she had her own views, but she wasn't foolish enough to try airing them in company.

Mrs Kington looked pointedly at the clock. 'We should be leaving,' she said, 'I must take no chances with Virginia's health, not after the alarms she caused us this morning.'

'Indeed not,' her friend replied. 'Howard, ring the bell and order the carriage.'

Virginia was silent as they were carried home through the dark foggy streets, glad that her companion didn't speak, because her head was full of Simon. Her interest hadn't gone unnoticed, but Mrs Kington said nothing until they were indoors.

'Mr Simon Roper is a personable young man,' the older woman said, once they were alone again in Virginia's sitting room, 'although I cannot approve of the escapade that brought him to our door. Nor do I care much for his choice of profession. It would have been better if his uncle had sent him into the law, or the church; either of which would provide a better position in society. Journalism is not quite suitable for a gentleman, and the *City Examiner* has a tendency to publicize issues which are best left alone.'

'I don't agree,' Virginia said spiritedly. 'I am not a fool. Although I haven't read the articles Mr Cardew mentioned, I know what he was talking about, and I think Mr Roper is right to draw attention to the plight of children who are mis-treated. While the fate of girls forced into immoral acts is swept quietly under the carpet, nothing will be done to help them.'

'Really, Virginia!' Mrs Kington recoiled. 'It is totally unacceptable for a young lady to speak of such matters, I am deeply shocked.'

'I believe my cousin would give them his wholehearted support if he were here.'

'He may well do,' Mrs Kington replied sourly. 'That doesn't make it a suitable subject of debate among decent people. Certain questions must be restricted to male conversations. They might properly be addressed in Parliament and the courts if necessary, but I don't believe they have any place in respectable households.'

'But the politicians and judges are quite happy to leave things as they are,' Virginia argued. 'I see a newspaper proprietor like Mr Roper as a

104

crusader, willing to fight to right wrongs that other people ignore.'

'I wonder if you would be so enthusiastic about the Press if Mr Roper hadn't brought his nephew with him tonight,' Mrs Kington said drily. 'However, the family are well connected, and he had the good sense to remain silent at the supper table when Mr Cardew made his unsavoury remarks. As long as he comports himself equally well in the future, I shan't discourage your cousin from including young Mr Roper in the invitation when he asks his friend to dine.' With this amazing concession, she bade Virginia goodnight.

Preparing for bed, Virginia dismissed Agnes as soon as she could, wanting to be alone with her thoughts. How different Mrs Kington's reaction would have been had she known the truth about her first meeting with Simon! And that she had every hope of seeing him again, and involving herself further in his work. By now he should have read her letter. What would he do? Perhaps he would refuse to meet her. She had planned with such care, but he might think her too calculating, maybe even unfeminine. Virginia extinguished her lamp, but it was a long time before she slept.

'A pretty young woman,' Jocelyn Roper remarked, as he led the way into his study, motioning to his nephew to pour from the decanter of port which stood ready for them. 'She didn't contribute a great deal to the conversation, but perhaps that was because of her evident preoccupation.'

'Her manners were perfect,' Simon replied hotly, handing his uncle a glass. 'And *pretty* is a rather insipid adjective. She's beautiful.'

Jocelyn smiled. 'I'm glad to see her fascination with you is not unrequited, it would be sad to see such devotion wasted. I confess that when we met at church this morning I suspected her of being rather dull.'

'Dull?' Simon bit down on an angry retort and took his own drink to the hearth, where he stood staring into the flames. 'How can you say such a thing? She's brave and clever. In fact, she's the finest girl I ever saw.'

'It was obvious that you thought so,' Jocelyn replied. 'Anyway, I revised my opinion. Any girl who can pass a billet-doux at the supper table with such aplomb has my approval, I am quite certain nobody else saw the transaction. I was disappointed to find the note was not meant for me, however, the initial is clearly an S, not a J.' He reached a hand into his pocket. 'I think you are a lucky young man. I only hope Sir Mortimer approves of you.'

Simon swung round, reaching to take the letter, but his uncle didn't immediately relinquish his hold on it.

'Perhaps I shouldn't condone such rash behaviour,' Jocelyn said. 'It might not be wise to allow an unattached young woman to send notes to my equally unattached young nephew.'

'Sir, if that letter is addressed to me,' Simon began, 'I should...' He met his uncle's eyes, and was amazed to see that the older man was finding it hard to restrain his laughter; in all the years they had been together, Jocelyn Roper had never indulged in teasing.

106

'I am sorry, my boy,' Jocelyn said, handing over the letter, 'I'm afraid I couldn't resist twitting you a little. Miss Bantry seems to have sharp wits, though they were kept in check in this evening's company, and I should say she has made up her mind where you are concerned. I doubt if her guardian will stand in her way.' His lips twitched. 'Indeed, I doubt if he would succeed if he attempted it. Open your letter, I shan't interrupt. Unless you'd prefer to wait until you are alone, to spare your blushes.'

Ignoring this fresh gibe, Simon fetched a knife from the desk and slit open the note. Courteously, Jocelyn went to stand by the fire, leaving his nephew some privacy, but in less than a minute the young man was at his side, his face flushed. 'A moment ago I told you that Miss Bantry has no faults, but it seems I'm mistaken. She thinks herself our ally, and has been spending her time spying on her neighbours. Among other things, she tells me there has been a man loitering in Lucas Place, and she suspects him of being associated with Mudd; that was foolhardy enough, since he might have observed her, but not content with that, she went to the cellar again! How could she be so rash?' He read on, an ever-deepening line appearing between his brows, until he looked closer in age to his uncle than to the girl who had written these words.

'What else?' Jocelyn asked.

'She saw a closed carriage go by and, having caught sight of a child's hand at the window, she has convinced herself that it was a girl being held against her will. Miss Bantry thought she should attempt another rescue. How could she commit such a folly?'

'Yet she returned safely; we saw her only an hour ago,' his uncle reminded him. 'The young lady continues to surprise me. Presumably her search was fruitless.'

'She was prevented from finding her way to that hell-hole by Sir Mortimer's butler, Willshire, who chose to enter the cellars just after she did. Abandoning her original plan, she followed him to another exit, one that took him out into daylight.'

'Does she link the butler with the attack that was made on you?'

'No. On that she seems clear. He went nowhere near the place where I was held.' The scowl on Simon's face deepened.

'Is there more?' his uncle prompted.

'The very worst. The foolish child proposes to try again. Not only does she intend to explore this new exit, but she still hopes to return to the place where I was being held, and try to find out what lies above it. What am I going to do?' He looked at the clock. 'It's far too late to call on her, and I could barely begin to explain all this to that gorgon who watches over her, but God knows what might happen if she starts wandering about the cellars again tonight!'

'She does seem a little headstrong,' Jocelyn agreed mildly.

'Headstrong!' Simon scanned the last few lines of the letter, then let out a long slow breath. 'It seems I needn't worry for the moment. Despite her fears for this child she will postpone her search until we have had a chance to talk. She'll be walking in the park tomorrow afternoon, and asks me to meet her. She points out that she'll have less freedom once Sir Mortimer arrives home on Wednesday, so her plan must be executed within the next two days.' He flung the letter down and ran his hand through his hair.

'A most unusual young woman,' Jocelyn observed, a slight smile on his lips. 'I confess I thought she had merely sent you a declaration of her affection.'

'She closes pleasantly,' Simon growled, 'but she is far too eager to involve herself with this business. I shall have to see her. I'm not sure I should wait until this proposed rendezvous – maybe I should call at the house tomorrow morning. We can't allow her to put herself at risk again.'

'She's given her word to do nothing until you meet, so I doubt that's necessary,' Jocelyn said. 'We have an appointment with Mrs Marchant, don't forget. Still, I should be interested to hear what else Miss Bantry has to say. I wonder what Sir Mortimer's butler was up to? And the other man, the one she claims is watching Lucas Place; didn't you mention somebody loitering on the street outside her house when you left with the doctor?'

'There was a man holding the horse; he answers her description.'

'She is unusually observant, for one so young.'

'You sound as if you approve of her meddling,' Simon said hotly. 'I accept that her motives are good, but no decent young woman should involve herself in such sordid matters.'

Jocelyn studied his nephew, his eyebrows raised

in interrogation. 'Has this letter revised your opinion of Miss Bantry so completely? Only minutes ago you were extolling her virtues. I agree she is most unusual for one of her sex, but not every civilized country treats their women as if they were weak and inferior beings, and those more open-minded cultures survive every bit as well as ours. Has she placed herself beyond the pale?'

Simon made a noise that was almost a groan. 'I hardly know what to think.'

'Then think of this,' Jocelyn replied, his voice firm. 'Had it not been for Miss Virginia Bantry's courage, and what you would call her unfeminine behaviour, I might still be waiting for you to return home, not knowing that you were dead, and your body floating in the Thames.'

Chapter Ten

With some reluctance, Simon accompanied his uncle to Mayfair, where they presented themselves at the smart London residence of Mr and Mrs Marchant.

Their hostess was a surprise; she was younger than he had expected, perhaps thirty years old, and her face, while strong in character, was exceedingly beautiful. There was a coolness in her manner as Jocelyn introduced him, and Simon acknowledged that the older man's judgement had been right; this woman was well aware of the effect her appearance had on men, and she

110

wouldn't be impressed by youthful good looks, or an appeal to pity.

'I thought I had already made myself clear,' she said, when they had explained their wish to interview some of the young women rescued by the Magdalene Home. 'It would not be appropriate. Those we help must be removed from the temptations which led them to stray in the first place; encounters with men are kept to a minimum. Even when a girl is genuinely repentant and wishes to redeem her good character, insofar as that is possible, we try to find her a position where she won't run the risk of being lured back into her old ways.'

'But if she was tricked or forced into her trade,' Simon said, 'surely she would have no wish to return to it.'

'Mr Roper, I doubt if one of these women would not claim to have been beguiled or misled into taking the first step on the downward slope. We have no time to apportion blame or listen to excuses; nor can we concern ourselves with the circumstances of individual cases. By the time they reach us, street women are inured to the lewd and corrupt ways of their trade. We bring them to an awareness of their sins, and offer them a way to a better life.'

'Yet through your offices a small child was rescued from a bawdy house,' Jocelyn Roper put in. 'You accept that very young girls are innocent victims in some cases.'

'That particular child was innocent,' Mrs Marchant said, 'but such incidences are unusual. I have read your editorials, Mr Roper. You make much of an evil which is extremely rare in this country. Male appetites, when uncontrolled and exercised outside the sanctity of the marriage bed, have led to the downfall of a great many women, but I fail to see why any man would choose to debauch a child. It is not natural. To my knowledge there is no organized trade in young girls, although some may join the profession at an early age.'

Simon was surprised to see his uncle making no attempt to dispute this sweeping statement, but, bowing his head in evident agreement, he said, 'I have no wish to argue with you. It was kind of you to allow us to see your records, and I shan't trouble you any more over the matter. But there is one thing I would ask. The man who told you where to find that child, the one you fetched out of the bawdy house. Would you help me to trace him?'

'I see no harm in that. His name is Higgs, and you are likely to find him among the traders at Lowe Street market.'

'She genuinely believes that all the guilt lies with the women,' Jocelyn said, as the two men made their way towards Lowe Street, leaving behind the gracious mansions of the gentry, 'as does all the disgrace, of course.'

'You aren't of the same mind?' Simon asked. 'I suppose if a woman has to choose between starving or selling her body, then we can understand that she might weaken, and be willing to fall into debauchery.'

'I doubt if the decision is always so clear cut.' Jocelyn frowned. 'Historically, there was a time

112

when girls of ten were considered mature enough to marry. These days, those who are wealthy enough to keep daughters well clothed and fed are happy to extend their childhood several years further than that, but willingly employ young children from the lower classes, and treat them little better than slaves. The main problem, it seems to me, is the vast gulf that separates the poor from the rest of humanity. Along with lack of understanding comes the reluctance to change. There are those who believe that if we educate the masses they will mend their ways, but that alone won't lift them out of the degradation that exists in the slums and warrens that still fester in London, despite the removal of the rookeries. As one area is cleared and rebuilt, so another slides down into greater poverty.'

'Maybe it's impossible to change the whole of society,' Simon said. 'As for the girls you hope to help, even with the facts before their eyes, people may refuse to see the truth.'

'That should not prevent us from trying,' Jocelyn replied. 'What we don't start can never be finished, and we will start with Higgs. I believe he was once employed by the men we're after. I can only think that his conscience pricked him when he encountered this small child. He sent a message to Mrs Marchant, in the hands of a woman she'd had some dealings with before; I'm hoping the jingle of a few coins might loosen his tongue.'

The first stallholder they approached pointed out a man with grizzled hair who was selling kindling, spills and tallow candles from a ramshackle barrow. As they turned in his direction the man watched them warily.

'Mr Higgs?' Jocelyn queried, his gaze roving over the man's wares as if he intended to make a purchase.

'Tha's me. But I got nuffin' to say. Unless you wants to buy, then move on, an' quick.'

'Nothing to say? Not even if it's worth five guineas to you?'

Higgs dropped his voice, shooting a sideways look at the bandage on Simon's hand. 'I seen you wiv 'er, the Magdalene woman, an' I knows what you're about. This young shaver's bin pokin' 'is nose in where it ain't wanted. Tha's a fool's game, an' I ain't no fool. A man can't work wiv 'is flipper in a sling, an' money ain't no good to nobody once 'e's floatin' dahn the river feedin' the bleedin' fish.'

'You told Mrs Marchant about a child in a bawdy house,' Jocelyn persisted. 'Thanks to you she was rescued before she was harmed. How did you know she was there?'

'Ain't nuffin' to tell. I 'eard it, tha's all.'

'But I think you've heard of a man called Mudd.' Jocelyn brought a handful of coins from his pocket. 'This could be yours. All I want is the name of the man Mudd works for.'

'You want too bleedin' much. I don' know no Mudd, an' if I did I wouldn' tell you 'oo he worked fer. Could be there's a gent involved, a right nob, an' it ain't worth tanglin' wiv 'im.' He gave the money a reluctant look then shook his head.

'Six guineas,' Jocelyn noted, as if reluctant to put the money away. He was surprised that his nephew had played no part in the conversation; a different approach might sway Higgs's resolve. 'A

114

word, that's all I'm after, and nobody will know where it came from.'

Simon had actually heard very little of the exchange between the other two men. His attention was fastened on a man lounging against a wall close to a stall selling cheap pots. Shielded by Higgs, he watched as the man icily scanned the crowded market.

'You already took a risk,' Jocelyn persisted, 'when you laid information about that child. How can this be any worse?'

Higgs spun back to him, looking alarmed. 'They don' know that was me.' He dropped his voice. 'I took a few messages, seein' as I gets to know the footmen an' 'ousekeepers, when I goes deliverin' to the big 'ouses. I 'elp out like, put 'em in touch. But tha's all. I don' 'old wiv 'em takin' them littluns. 'Tain't right. I got a kid o' me own, see.'

'But this man specializes in young children,' Jocelyn pointed out.

'I wouldn' know. Tha's nuffin' to do wi' me. Sling yer 'ook, mister, an' leave me alone.' Higgs turned his back on them, suddenly intent upon his wares.

'Damn,' Simon muttered, lowering his head as he followed his uncle across the street. 'Don't let the rogue see you, sir, but look at the man in a ragged hat, by the pot stall. I swear he's the one who held the doctor's horse the other morning, the one Miss Bantry wrote about.'

'But why would he be loitering in Lowe Street?' Jocelyn said, taking a quick look before turning away. 'Unless it's you he's interested in.'

'Or our friend Higgs,' Simon said. They were in

115

the middle of a deeper crowd, gathered around a one-armed man who was giving a display of dexterity and strength with his remaining hand. 'Why don't we ask him? If you'd wait for a moment, sir, and keep your eyes on him, I'll let him get a good look at me. Assuming he'll follow, you can come along behind. Once we're out of this crush we'll have him between us.'

Before Jocelyn could protest, Simon was gone, and there was nothing to do but obey his suggestion, although not without a certain amount of irritation. The boy's hand would be a severe handicap if it came to a fight, and as proprietor of the *City Examiner*, he couldn't afford to involve himself in a public brawl. For a moment the tall, soldierly man didn't move. Jocelyn made a faint impatient sound; obviously the man was simply a loiterer with too much time on his hands. He was about to follow his nephew when the man suddenly lunged into motion, going directly towards the passageway where Simon had gone.

Jocelyn crossed the street, his long legs propelling him a little faster than his usual leisurely pace. Slowing as he entered the comparative darkness of the narrow alley, Jocelyn strained to make out the single dark shape silhouetted ahead of him.

'Where did he go?' Simon asked, hurrying back towards his uncle. 'Was I wrong, didn't he come this way?'

'I thought I'd find him here,' Jocelyn said, staring at the smoke-blackened walls on either side. There was a narrow gap that might once have been a doorway, though the bricks above and beside it looked ready to fall at any moment.

116

Inside there was a yawning blackness and a thick stench. 'You have an answer to your question. He was watching you, and he's a great deal more professional about his craft than we are.'

As Simon made to climb through the gap Jocelyn stopped him, taking a firm grip on his elbow. 'No. He's on his own territory here, and may well have friends to call on. We'll keep our eyes open, and try again when we have the advantage.'

'But he can't be far away,' Simon said, staring into the gloom in frustration.

'All the more reason to be cautious. Do I have to remind you that your recklessness already left you with a broken hand? You're hardly in a shape to defend yourself in a brawl.'

'Seeing Higgs was a waste of time, and Mrs Marchant refuses help,' Simon said. 'We know this man is connected with the affair somehow, we shouldn't let him get away.'

'I think maybe Higgs told us something, even if he didn't mean to,' Jocelyn said, slowly leading the way back to Lowe Street. 'Why would Mudd need a man who regularly calls at respectable households, and has contacts with housekeepers and footmen?'

'I don't know.' Simon was distracted, his thoughts still upon the man who had vanished so expertly.

'Perhaps they advise him of suitable young girls who might be snatched without risk of reprisal. Some households are slack in the management of their servants. Wasn't there some mention of one of Mrs Marchant's fallen women having argued with a housekeeper, and been persuaded by the footman to take up another post, only to find she had moved into a brothel?'

'Maybe,' Simon said, though he still wasn't paying attention. Abruptly he stopped in his tracks, as if stricken. 'If that man who was watching us is working with Mudd, they know I'm alive. They will have worked out that I had help to escape, that somebody else was involved. Mudd could be looking for Virginia at this very moment.'

Having squeezed through the gap in the bricks and felt his way through to a rickety staircase, guided more by memory than any of his senses, the tall man climbed, feeling the rotten treads tremble beneath his feet, climbing three storeys before he came to a halt. He was certain he had lost the two men who had shown such unwanted interest in him; he knew these warrens like the back of his hand, and only a fool would attempt to follow him here.

A broken door to his left let in a sliver of light, and he pushed through it. The floor here had fallen away, only a few half-rotten joists stretching across to the outer wall. With barely a moment's hesitation he ran across to the window, finding a slightly safer foothold close to the wall, and leaning on the rickety sill. Looking down, he spotted the two men easily; they were better dressed than most of the crowd milling around the market-stalls. They had abandoned the chase as he hoped; the older of the two seemed intent only on threading a way through the crowds and heading west, but the younger, the one with the injured arm, was looking about him, stopping now and then and letting his gaze rove over the buildings that lined Lowe Street. The tall man drew back, hiding in the deeper shadows.

A long moment passed, then the two men moved on; very soon they would be out of sight. Turning, the tall man realized he wasn't alone. An old crone, dressed in rags, and with a blanket wrapped tight around her shrivelled frame, was crouched on the floor in the corner of the room, where a small patch of floorboards remained in place. The man wasn't sure she was alive; the smell of death hung in the ruined room, but she opened bloodshot eyes and mumbled something as he walked the narrow way back to the door. He paused, and reached into his pocket for a coin. 'For luck,' he said, tossing it to her. The old woman snatched it from the air, only to sink once more into her apparent stupor.

The tall man ran back down the rickety stairs, feeling his way, eager to get on the tail of his quarry again, before they had time to disappear.

'Would I be right in thinking you have some particular reason for taking a walk today?' Mrs Yelding asked, tucking her arm comfortably within Virginia's as they stepped into the street and turned towards the park.

Virginia flushed. 'I do hope to meet an acquaintance, though I'm not depending on it.'

'But doubtless you made sure this acquaintance would know where to find you.' The older woman patted Virginia's hand. 'I quite understand. The park is much more suitable than your parlour, especially with Mrs Kington in the house, and all the preparations for your uncle's return turning things upside down.' They walked in companionable silence for a few moments. 'I gather you met our newest neighbour, Reverend Solcott.'

'Yes. He knows Sir Mortimer, I imagine that's why he asked to be introduced.'

'You underestimate yourself.' Mrs Yelding sighed. 'Eighteen years old, not only pretty but eligible, any young man would be eager for an introduction. And equally eager to arrange a second meeting,' she added slyly.

'He refused our invitation to tea,' Virginia said, 'because he was going away to visit a sick friend. I don't expect to see him for several days.'

'So he is not the lucky man. I have guessed wrongly.'

'I didn't say my acquaintance was a man,' Virginia said quickly.

'I am a woman of the world, my dear; twice widowed.' Mrs Yelding's bright eyes gave her a searching look. 'I know Mrs Kington's rule has been a little too rigorous at times, but I must ask whether your cousin would approve of this assignation.'

'I admit I hope to meet a young man, but Sir Mortimer is already acquainted with his uncle, Mr Jocelyn Roper, who is proprietor of the *City Examiner*. When we met, Mr Roper assured me he would introduce his nephew to Sir Mortimer, as soon as he returns.'

They turned in at the park gates. 'Roper,' Mrs Yelding repeated. 'I believe I know that family. There was some tragedy I think, an accident. Your young man lives with his uncle?'

'Yes.' Virginia blushed. 'But he isn't my young man. At the moment we have interests in common, that's all. We only wish to talk.'

'I see no harm in that. There is a seat which gives an excellent view of the path around the pond. If you and Mr Roper wish to walk, I may find myself in need of a little rest.'

Virginia thanked her, and was saved from having to say more by the sight of Simon Roper coming towards them. He was immaculately dressed, and had his bandaged hand tucked discreetly into the front of his waistcoat.

With the introductions over, they walked half a circuit of the pond, then Mrs Yelding, as good as her word, arranged herself on the bench. 'I shall watch the ducks,' she said, 'and anything else which offers to be of interest.' By this, Virginia understood that she and Simon would be under observation. She could feel the now-familiar tingle running through her body at Simon's nearness, as if her blood was more than usually warm.

They walked side by side, a decorous distance always between them. Glancing sideways she met his eyes and, realized that his problem was no less than hers. Virginia's mouth quirked in a small smile. If this was love it made having a sensible conversation very difficult.

'You went back to the cellar,' he said abruptly. 'Promise you'll never to do it again.'

'Don't worry. I was quite safe, and I saw nothing, except my cousin's butler.'

'You were lucky, but there's no reason to suppose your good fortune will hold if you take such a risk again.' He turned to face her, forcing her to stop walking. 'You could be in real danger. The tall man, the one you mentioned in your letter; he was there that morning, in Lucas Place. I suspect he's working with Mudd, and apparently he's watching both of us. They could already have discovered how I escaped.'

'I don't see–' she began, but he wasn't listening.

'He may have seen me leave your house!' Simon's face was anguished. Even as he spoke he noticed a ragged-looking individual, half hidden among some bushes. The man wore a filthy shapeless hat, exactly like the one he had seen in Lowe Street only hours before.

Chapter Eleven

'I should never have agreed to meet you,' Simon said, risking a glance at the villain who was shadowing him, wanting to run and confront the man. He couldn't desert Virginia; their meeting had been a mistake. 'I'll escort you back to your friend, and then you must go home and stay indoors. We shouldn't be here together.'

'Whatever do you mean?' She turned her head, looking for the cause of his disquiet. 'What's the matter?'

'Don't look that way. There's a man over there. Surely he's the one who was outside your house, the one you say is haunting Lucas Place.'

Disobeying his order not to look, Virginia lifted onto tiptoes to get a clearer view of the path paralleling their own. 'No, that doesn't look like the same man, not a bit. The one who has been loitering in Lucas Place is very upright and brisk, like an old soldier. That poor soul is bent almost double, and he can barely shuffle along.'

'Are you sure? If he wanted to disguise himself then he might walk differently. I saw the man only hours ago, I'd swear that's him.'

'I don't see why you are so worried,' Virginia said. 'Even if you are right, and he is watching us, what can he do, out here in the open, surrounded by all these people?'

'How can you be so trusting? Suppose he was carrying a knife, or a gun.' His good hand ran compulsively across the back of his neck. 'I can't bear to think of anything happening to you. Don't you see now how wrong it is for you to be involved in all this?'

'I'm not nearly as delicate as you imagine,' Virginia protested. 'As for that poor old man carrying a gun, like some foreign assassin, the whole idea is ridiculous.'

'Maybe.' He stared down into her face, relishing her nearness yet wishing himself gone from there. 'I only know that I couldn't live with myself if anything were to happen to you.'

'Nothing is going to happen. We should walk,' Virginia said, her voice only a little shaky with the unaccustomed emotions that racked her. They went on, the air between them charged with their unspoken awareness of each other.

'Talk to me, Mr Roper, I beg you,' Virginia said at last. 'Help me regain my composure. Tell me what you know about this awful trade in chil-

123

dren. Please,' she added hurriedly, seeing the doubt on his face. 'Don't insult me by speaking of the weather, the least you can do is help me understand what is going on. I am hardly likely to forget how we met; that man from the cellar will haunt me until I know he has been apprehended.'

'But you must forget,' Simon said. 'And you mustn't get involved any further.'

Virginia's chin lifted in a gesture Mrs Kington would have recognized all too well. 'I have no wish to be wrapped in cotton wool like a china doll, and kept safe and protected in a stuffy drawing room. Beneath these clothes, behind the veneer of the manners drummed into me by my decent upbringing, I am made of the same flesh and blood as the poor women whose children have been stolen from them. You seem to have very little recollection of what happened that night. If you had heard that evil man, talking of *pieces of merchandise* as if they were no more than bales of cloth, or sacks of coal, perhaps you would understand.'

'You think I have no sympathy for those he has wronged, that my uncle and I are only interested in selling more copies of the *Examiner?*' Simon shot back. 'We believe in what we are doing, but I cannot condone your interference any further, not when it puts you at risk. You're a woman,' he concluded, as if that should settle the matter.

'So I am interfering?' She spoke quietly, yet there was a warning in her tone. 'It is because I'm a woman that I want these awful men to be punished for what they have done. I can't stop thinking about that night. There was talk of two children being brought to him, by Mrs Harper,

124

or Harding, or Harwood.' She shook her head in frustration. 'It was none of those. If only I could remember it might help you. I'm sure if I heard it again it would be familiar to me.'

'I'd rather you thought no more about it. I wish you were safe, a hundred miles away.'

Ignoring this, Virginia went on, 'Thanks to Cook, who collects newspapers for the fire, I was able to read one of your uncle's editorials. It's all horrible, unthinkable, but I need to know more. I promise I shan't swoon away.'

Simon was still reluctant. 'It isn't a subject to discuss out in the open.'

'Nor anywhere else apparently,' she said. 'This is ridiculous. We shall soon enter a new century, Mr Roper, the whole world lies open to men, yet women must sit in their parlours, playing the piano and reading novels. Not me. I may have to wait a little while for my freedom, but one day I shall break out of my prison.'

Virginia glanced at him, remembering the plan that had taken her into the cellar in the first place. The suit of clothes she had collected with such toil and secrecy was hidden in her bedroom. If her cousin deserted her again, she would find a way to leave the house whenever she pleased, dressed as a man, and explore the parts of the city which were forbidden her. Simon was walking beside her, evidently lost in thought. What would he make of her scheme? The feelings she had for him could not be denied, but she couldn't face a future with Simon Roper if he wanted to trap her in a gilded cage.

'I'd never really considered this before,' he said

at last. 'I'd always imagined that women were completely different, that they wouldn't share my concerns. But now I realize it must be hard, with all your spirit and intelligence, to be constrained by the rules and strictures that society places on you. My uncle told me as much, and I didn't understand what he was trying to say, but I have to acknowledge that without your help I would probably be dead.'

Virginia murmured a polite protest, although she was inclined to agree with him.

He waved her half-hearted objection aside. 'Perhaps society has grown too protective. I have met and written about women who are strong and independent. They have always had to fight for their freedom and then they are judged to be unfeminine, I was guilty of seeing them that way, even while I admired their achievements. I have no right to tell you what to do, or think; I only know that I can't bear the thought of seeing you in danger.'

After this speech it took Virginia a moment to find her voice. Determinedly setting aside his last words, although they were the ones that meant the most to her, she avoided meeting his eyes when she finally replied; that way lay a chaos which she knew she wasn't yet prepared for. 'Hearing a little more about this business can't endanger me. Tell me what first led you to Mudd.'

With a visible effort Simon drew a little away from her, studying the tree-lined walk as if it was of intense interest to him. The bent man in the tattered hat had gone; perhaps she had been right and the likeness to the watcher had only existed in his imagination. 'You aren't the only one having trouble remembering things; I'm afraid that knock on the head left a great many gaps in my memory.'

'Perhaps talking about it will help,' she said.

He sighed. 'I saw a large man in the company of a person I knew had some small part in the kidnapping of a child; it was really a stab in the dark. Since there was nothing more to learn from the original contact, when they separated I followed the big brute, and he led me to Newscombe Street. There was an urchin sleeping in the gateway to the mews, and he was willing to talk to me for the sake of a penny. He told me the man's name was Mudd, and I paid him to carry a message to my uncle, asking that he join me. I had some idea of walking around Lucas Place, but even then I suspected that I'd been noticed.' He pulled a wry face. 'Obviously I was right.'

'But your uncle didn't come.'

'He could make nothing of my note.' Simon gave a rueful smile. 'That's about all I remember. I know I lost sight of Mudd, and after that it's a blank. The next thing that has any relation to reality was waking up and seeing you.'

'Don't you remember the other man, the one who questioned you?' Virginia shivered. 'He had the voice of a gentleman, but no gentleman would have spoken as he did.'

'It's like a nightmare. He was a demon in the dark, a voice making threats, that's all. I can't recall what he said, and I don't remember seeing his face, only that he wore dark clothes. Perhaps if I met him again it would jog my memory and help me to recognize him.'

'I hope you never do,' Virginia said vehemently.

He gave her a look which made her falter in her tracks, and she fixed her gaze away from him again, lifting a hand to wave at Mrs Yelding on the other side of the pond.

'We really need to find out more about the cellars under Lucas Place,' she said, 'if you won't let me explore them, how are we to do it?'

'My uncle has made enquiries about your neighbours,' Simon said, taking his cue from her, and returning doggedly to business. 'He has learnt that Reverend Solcott comes from a respectable family, that he is an orphan, and that he had a living near Liverpool for over a year before he came here. As for Mr Jeffrey Parkin, he was at Oxford until recently, but it is believed that he has returned to London.'

'Really? Then we have a possible suspect.'

'Maybe. Though if he is living with his father he has become as reclusive as the old man,' Simon said. 'He's not been seen. Don't you have any suspicion of Reverend Solcott? Not all clergymen are irreproachable.'

'I did have some doubts,' Virginia admitted, 'until I saw him in church, and heard him preach. He is very much the gentleman, but his voice is higher and more carrying than that of the man in the cellar, and I've never seen anyone with a more open and honest face.'

'An innocent face is a great asset to a rogue,' Simon observed.

Virginia shook her head. 'I simply can't imagine him doing anything that might harm a child, or

128

speaking so casually of death, as that man did in the cellar.'

'From what little I remember those cellars seem quite remarkable,' Simon said. 'Do you know who built them?'

'My cousin thinks the oldest passageways are Roman,' Virginia replied, 'and that they were extended hundreds of years later, when a church or monastery was built on the site.'

'I'd like a chance to take a proper look. Old maps might prove useful, perhaps I can find a record of the entrance your butler used.' Simon's voice drifted into silence. They would soon have completed their circuit and his chance to speak would be lost. He stopped and faced her. 'You must tell me, do you feel what I feel? I hardly slept, thinking about you.'

'Hush,' Virginia said urgently, stepping round him and walking on, so he was forced to follow. 'If we once allow ourselves to say such things, how are we ever to meet? Mrs Yelding is a good soul, but she is a notorious gossip, and she won't be able to resist telling Mrs Kington if our feelings become too obvious.'

This time he groaned aloud. 'You yourself said you hate the restraints society places on you. Miss Bantry, you must know how I feel, and what I ask. Why do we have to be bound by stupid conventions? Will you–?'

'Hush,' she repeated, though her heart was singing; at that fleeting moment she thought she had only to spread her arms and she would fly like a bird. 'Don't say it. Not yet. We won't have to wait long. When Sir Mortimer returns, your uncle will introduce you to him. I doubt if my cousin will raise any objections to...' She faltered, lowering her eyes. She wasn't quite audacious enough to say the words she'd forbidden him to utter. 'Mrs Kington has given a slightly cautious approval of you already, and I'm sure he'll accept her recommendation. We have to be patient, that's all.'

All too soon they were rejoining Mrs Yelding. 'When exactly do you expect Sir Mortimer to return?' Simon asked.

'On Wednesday, unless his boat is delayed,' Virginia replied with apparent calm.

'I am sure my uncle will call upon him very soon.' Simon took Mrs Yelding's hand. 'Mrs Yelding, I am so glad to have met you.'

'Oh, I don't doubt this will only be the first of many meetings,' the woman said, her cheeks dimpling. 'I find it quite pleasant to have young company for a walk at about this time each day. Virginia is a dear friend, and I have her interests very much at heart.'

'Then we have something in common straight away,' Simon replied. He made a move as if to take Virginia's hand, then drew back as if the contact might scorch him. 'Miss Bantry.' He bowed and walked briskly away.

'A shared interest,' Mrs Yelding chuckled, as the two women began their leisurely stroll home, 'that is a most apposite phrase.'

Virginia's exalted state had left her. She felt deflated, and very tired, as if she had been out in the fresh air all day, rather than a mere hour. 'Don't tease me,' she begged. 'I have met Mr Roper only twice before today. I thought ... I don't

130

know what I thought.'

'That you might not feel the same way when you saw him again? That you had imagined what happened before?' Mrs Yelding shook her head gravely. 'My dear, your emotions are written clearly in your eyes, and mirrored on the face of that young man.'

Mercifully the woman was silenced at that point, for they had reached the main road, where the noise of the traffic made conversation difficult. Virginia, hardly aware of her surroundings, followed meekly in Mrs Yelding's footsteps, accepting her offer of tea, grateful that she had time to calm herself before she had to face Mrs Kington.

Walking through the hall some time later, Virginia could hear Willshire haranguing the new manservant, his voice echoing all the way from the pantry, and the meals were so far out of their normal routine that tea was only just being served to Mrs Kington as she arrived. Agnes slammed the tray on the table before running off again, her face like thunder.

'Forgive me,' Virginia said, briefly joining her companion, 'I fear I am already quite full of tea, having been obliged to keep Miss Forswick company for a full hour.'

'I can drink none of it either,' Mrs Kington replied. 'I have a headache and I am going directly to my room. Please ring for Agnes to remove the tray. And tell her I require a cup of camomile tea, to be brought upstairs at once.'

'All this pother and flurry,' Agnes declared, when Virginia had relayed Mrs Kington's orders. 'If there's nothing else you want then, Miss Virginia?'

'Nothing, thank you,' Virginia said, although in reality there was a great deal she wanted, none of it within anybody's gift, unless perhaps that of her cousin, Sir Mortimer. It was strange to think that he would be here soon; she had looked forward to his coming for months, but so much had happened in the last few days that now she barely knew what to wish for. She felt she had been changed, inside and out, completely transfigured by the arrival of Simon Roper until she barely recognized herself.

Sir Mortimer had always treated her with great kindness, but suppose he didn't care so much for this new Virginia? Or that he took a dislike to Simon? She must decide how much to reveal about her recent adventures; she had rarely kept secrets from her cousin, but she was reluctant to recount the whole story of Simon's rescue. Her cousin should be told about Willshire's unexplained knowledge of the underground labyrinth but it wouldn't be an easy subject to raise. Spying on a trusted servant was the height of bad manners; it would be best if she could find out what the butler had been up to, before Sir Mortimer came home.

Virginia made her way to the kitchen. Cook was busy, but seeing that her visitor looked unsettled, she found time to make her a hot milk drink, just as she had when Virginia was a lonely fourteen year old, new to London.

'I've never known Mr Willshire in such a mood,' Cook confided quietly. 'He nearly snapped my head off when I asked to have the fish pan lifted down from the top shelf. I told him, I'm not as young as I was, and where would Sir Mortimer be if he came home to find me in bed with a broken leg, if you please. A fine welcome he'd have, with no meals on the table, for he'd not find another cook at short notice, not in London at this time of year.'

'I hope Mr Willshire did as you asked,' Virginia replied.

'He told the new man to do it. I don't know, it wasn't like this in the old days, servants coming and going. When I was young, once a maid or a man had a place with a good family, they kept it, no matter what, as long as they behaved themselves.'

'Yes,' Virginia replied vaguely. 'I suppose they did.'

'I mean, look at poor Mrs Ross. Do you know they never even gave her time to come and say goodbye to her old friends? First I knew about it was from Mr Burrows's boy, when he came with the meat. Vanished she did, there one day and gone the next. And we can't keep a kitchen girl. There was Daisy, she was a bright little thing, a bit inclined to be cheeky, but we'd soon have cured her of that. And yet she hardly stayed long enough to learn where things were kept, and she'd gone.'

'I don't think Emily will leave,' Virginia said. 'I'm hoping my cousin will allow her to be trained as an upstairs maid, she's much more cheerful and willing than Agnes.'

'Well, I dare say Sir Mortimer might be persuaded, though I can't see Mr Willshire being too keen on the idea,' Cook said. She pushed Virginia gently out of her way as she carried a pie to the oven. 'He's sent her out in the yard to clean his boots, if you please, when I've got my hands full in here. We all have such a deal to do.'

'I'm sorry; I'll leave you to your work,' Virginia said. She wandered rather disconsolately into the front parlour, the only place not being turned upside down. She wished she could play some useful part in all the preparations for her cousin's return, even if it meant wielding a brush or a mop. The thought of Mrs Kington's reaction if she attempted such a thing brought a smile to her face, but it soon faded. Her thoughts were so unsettling, she couldn't bear to be still, yet she could find nothing to occupy her.

Virginia stood in the dismal little room and stared out of the window, wondering if she might see that closed carriage pass by again; within moments, although her eyes were fixed on the street, she was seeing nothing of the people passing by; her mind had turned back to her walk in the park. And Simon.

Chapter Twelve

'I should like you to remain here,' Jocelyn Roper said, eyeing his nephew across his desk. 'Looking back, allowing you to accompany me to Lowe Street was unwise. If you are right, and the man we saw is working with Mudd, then we can be sure the news of your survival will have reached these villains by now; Higgs is no fool, he might decide it's safer to run and tell his old master we're making enquiries, rather than risk him finding out from somebody else. If he mentions your injured hand they'll be sure to work out who you are.'

'I can't say that worries me, sir,' Simon replied. 'If they think we're getting too close for comfort perhaps they'll take action and give us something to take to the police.'

'Or, since they think you can identify Mudd and his master well enough to see them charged in a court of law, they may decide you have to be put permanently out of the way,' Jocelyn said, with some asperity. 'They don't know you are suffering from amnesia.'

'I'll do well enough as long as I keep clear of their haunts,' Simon said. 'They can hardly kidnap me in broad daylight. I am more concerned for Miss Bantry. I tried to persuade her to stay away from the cellars, but she refused to make any promises.'

'Her cousin returns home very soon, and with a man in the house to take care of her I'm sure she'll be perfectly safe,' Jocelyn said. 'And she doesn't go out unattended. It is only her connection with you that puts her in danger.'

'I know. I shouldn't have agreed to that assignation in the park. We're supposed to meet there again tomorrow afternoon.' Simon frowned. 'If I don't go she'll wonder why, but every time it increases the chance that Mudd or his henchmen will see us together.'

'Stay within doors for a few days, and I shall meet Miss Bantry for you,' Jocelyn said.

Simon stared at his uncle. 'You expect me not

to leave the house at all? Sir, I agree to keep well clear of Miss Bantry, though I hate the necessity, and I'll stay away from the area around Lucas Place, but I refuse to make myself a prisoner.'

Jocelyn was silent for a long moment, his face grave. 'Simon, ever since the deaths of your parents I have been responsible for you, and I have never had cause to regret taking on that charge. For their sake, if not for mine, I hope you will respect my wishes. Tomorrow morning at eleven, I expect a visit from the police detective who has been investigating these kidnappings. I ask you to be here, and not to leave this house before that time. The inspector hopes that arrests will be made within a week.'

'I'm willing to talk to your tame policeman,' Simon said, 'but I refuse to lurk behind closed curtains like a frightened infant. There are still several lines of enquiry to be pursued, and I may be able to bring some new evidence to this meeting. I'll not be coddled and watched over, and I shan't skulk indoors while Virginia Bantry is at risk from these men.'

'Then you leave me no alternative.' Jocelyn Roper's face had taken on a tinge of pink; Simon had seen him lose his temper so rarely that he didn't recognize the danger sign. 'You ask me to treat you like an adult and yet you act with no more sense than a child of five.' He rose to his feet, glaring at his nephew, his voice rising to levels rarely heard in that quiet room. 'Since you refuse to co-operate willingly, I am ordering you not to leave this building until I give you permission. Is that clear?'

'Perfectly,' Simon said, his own temper flaring in response, and every bit as irreconcilable as his uncle's. He turned on his heel, dragging the office door open to run down the stairs and out of the front door, which slammed loudly behind him.

Virginia woke, the remnants of a cry on her lips. She lay staring into the darkness. It had taken her a long time to fall asleep, and then the old nightmare had crept into her dreams, as fresh and terrible as on its first visitation. The smell of that distant bazaar was still with her, an alien mixture of spices and sweat and animals, and the scent seemed almost to linger still, on the bed linen which clung damply to her body.

Throwing back the covers, Virginia drew her robe around her and went to the window to stare out at the night, trying to banish the images that were so vivid in her mind. Lit by the dim red horror of the African bordello, the open door had revealed not the carpet-draped walls of memory, but grey stone that dripped with damp, beneath a vaulted ceiling. As she peered into the shadows a dark shape writhed upon the floor, jerking with an urgent hypnotic rhythm; as always she could make out no detail, except that this time there was the spread of small fingers, stretching towards her in silent appeal as they shone white in the gloom.

Unable to wake, unable to move, Virginia had watched as the tiny fingers were enclosed in a huge dark hand, and dragged back into the heaving mass. She had cried out then, and mercifully her own voice had woken her.

Gradually Virginia's pounding heart slowed to

its normal beat, and she saw the haloes of mist around the gas lamps that lit Lucas Place, recognized the familiar outlines of the trees lining the other side of the square, and the tall buildings beyond. She knew why she had been visited by this old demon; convinced that the child in the carriage was bound for the cellar, her conscience pricked her. She had done nothing, ignoring that hand and its plea for help.

She shuddered. Simon had been so insistent that she must take no further risks. His distress haunted her, yet maybe, if only she had the courage, it wasn't too late to save that small lost innocent, even now.

Virginia grew cold, standing barefoot and half dressed in the draught that found its way through cracks around the window panes, but she made no move. Simon had called her courageous. Was the unknown child to be abandoned because of a bad dream?

Deeply ashamed, Virginia faced the truth. She dared not return to the cellar. Not this night and alone, not with the horror of the nightmare still upon her damp skin, like the caress of cold, dead fingers. At long last, shivering, she returned to her bed. In the morning she would find some way to act, though how she could not tell. Or perhaps she would ask Simon, when they met in the park; he would know what to do.

She listened to the clock in the hall as it chimed, marking off each quarter of an hour, through four o'clock, then five. It was almost six before her eyelids drooped wearily, and she sank once more into sleep.

The morning found Virginia tired and irritable, and the guilt she had suffered in the night hadn't lessened with the coming of day, Her renewed resolve would have sent her into the cellars that morning, but there was no hope of it with the house in uproar; there seemed to be servants and tradesmen everywhere. With only twenty-four hours left before Sir Mortimer's return, Willshire's black mood had worsened; he was driving the maids to tears, striding around the house with a face like thunder, and even Cook seemed reluctant to risk upsetting him further. It certainly wouldn't do to be found trespassing in his domain. Meaning only to assure herself that Mrs Yelding would accompany her to the park again that afternoon, Virginia escaped from the turmoil to visit her neighbours. Since she could see no likelihood of visiting the cellar she must rely on Simon Roper; she had told him about Willshire and the tunnel that led into daylight. With a slight lightening of her mood she persuaded herself that even now he could be discovering the way in.

'My dear, I'm so glad you called this morning,' Mrs Yelding said, smiling as she welcomed Virginia into her drawing room, eyes alight with excitement. 'I was afraid I might see nothing of you until our walk this afternoon, and I am just bursting to tell somebody our news. You will never guess who came to call, it was so unexpected, although of course, being so close, I suppose you may well guess correctly. He's only just left; had you been here five minutes earlier, you should have seen him yourself!'

Virginia wasn't in the mood for Mrs Yelding's

riddles, but she bit off the hasty reply that came to her lips. 'You've had a call from a neighbour? Virginia hazarded. 'Not Reverend Solcott? I thought he was to be away all week.'

'No, this was a nearer neighbour even than Reverend Solcott. It's such a coincidence, so soon after we were speaking of him,' Mrs Yelding said, 'Of course he was barely more than a boy when I saw him last, and you won't remember him at all, but although I didn't catch his name when little Maria announced him, I knew exactly who he was the moment he entered the room.' Perhaps becoming aware of Virginia's irritation she shook her head. 'I'm sorry, my dear, I shouldn't tease. It was Mr Jeffrey Parkin.'

'So he is at home!' Virginia's reaction was all Mrs Yelding could have wanted, and the elderly widow beamed.

'Indeed, I was just as surprised as you, my dear.' She went on to tell of the days when she and her sister first moved to Lucas Place, and how they had taken pity on the lonely boy next door. With no supervision from his father, the youngster's nurse had rarely bothered to take him out and about, and when the nurse was replaced by a tutor, things had been little better. Mr Parkin senior, even then, had kept entirely withdrawn, confining himself to his study and bedroom, never venturing downstairs. 'Young Jeffrey was always devoted to history, I remember, even as a small child. I suppose that is where this new interest began.'

Virginia was hardly listening, her thoughts following quite a different course; she need look no further to give a name to the smooth-voiced villain from the cellar. Had she been at Mrs Yelding's door a few minutes earlier, she might have heard him, and been quite sure. She suppressed a shudder, recalling the gentlemanly tone, so much at odds with the words the man had spoken.

'I was truly sorry to have to refuse his request,' Mrs Yelding was saying, 'it would be such a small thing, if it weren't for my sister's fears, but of course she wouldn't hear of it. I was very much surprised that the cellar below his father's house doesn't connect with ours, but he assures me it was all blocked off many years ago. Between you and me, his father was always a little strange, evidently he had walls built in the basement, in case his neighbours used the tunnels to find a way into his house. As if anyone would do such a thing.' She gave a little laugh, 'but then, I suppose, his fears are no more irrational than those of my poor sister, with her terror that deadly diseases lurk down below ground.'

'I'm sorry,' Virginia said, 'but I'm not sure I understand. Did you say Mr Jeffrey Parkin wanted to find a way in to your cellar?'

'Well, yes, that's right. Not just ours, but all of them. I don't know how he heard about the old chambers and tunnels, but he was quite excited about them. I always thought archaeology was all about Egyptian tombs and Greek temples, but obviously I was wrong. Apparently Roman remains are all the rage now.'

Virginia's thoughts were racing. She didn't believe Jeffrey Parkin was interested in Roman remains; he had invented the perfect excuse for

141

poking about in the passages under Lucas Place, to find out how Simon Roper had escaped from the cellar. Doubtless the impromptu prison was below his own house, and the story about his father having walled it up was a lie.

'It's odd that he has only developed this interest now,' she said. 'He must have known the Roman remains were there when he was living in Lucas Place as a boy.'

'I doubt if he did. The poor child was rarely free to roam about the house. I think his father was very hard on him, and I'm sure such an adventure wouldn't have been allowed.' Mrs Yelding leant closer, so she could whisper in Virginia's ear. 'Between you and me, old Mr Parkin is a complete invalid these days; our Polly is friendly with one of his nurses. She tells me he doesn't even know his own name, and his son is a total stranger to him. It's very sad. There was a time when the doctors feared that young Mr Parkin might have inherited his father's illness, but luckily he has taken more after his mother. I saw her portrait once, long ago; she was a pretty thing, though rather delicate perhaps. Certainly Mr Jeffrey has done well in his studies, and returns to us with letters after his name, and a certain amount of fame in the corridors of academe.'

'Really?' Mr Jeffrey Parkin might tell Mrs Yelding whatever he pleased, and his old friend and neighbour would believe him, but Virginia wasn't to be deflected by his tall tales. The young man might not have turned himself into a hermit, but in his case his father's malady had evidently taken a different course. It had turned him to a life of crime. There was no doubt in Virginia's mind: this man was a rogue and a liar, and he must be exposed before any more innocent children fell into his hands.

Hardly knowing how she kept her composure, Virginia managed to take leave of Mrs Yelding, with a promise that she hadn't forgotten their walk that afternoon.

Chapter Thirteen

Jocelyn Roper was openly watching the street, making no pretence of working. A familiar figure was crossing between the traffic, but it wasn't the one he wished to see; hearing his nephew return to the house in the early hours had brought only a temporary ease to his anxiety, for the boy hadn't sought him out, and had left again before breakfast.

Inspector Laker of London's detective division was lost to Jocelyn's sight as he approached the door. With no real hope that Simon would appear, Jocelyn took one last long look at the scene below, and then returned to his desk, ready to greet Inspector Laker. The policeman was an imposing figure, Jocelyn's equal in height but a good deal bulkier. Lowering himself into a seat, the inspector accepted the offer of the tobacco jar, silently filling his pipe with the attention the task deserved.

'It's probable you've made yourself a few more

'enemies, Mr Roper,' Laker said, once his pipe was well alight.

Jocelyn eyed him warily; he believed Laker to be an honest law officer, but it was possible that his superiors, influenced by the government minister or others of his kind, might try to put pressure upon him. He said nothing, waiting for the man to go on.

'I understand your nephew got himself into a fix he was lucky to get out of.'

'We'd hoped that wasn't generally known,' Jocelyn said. The fear that had been nagging at him since the previous evening was like a chill touch on his heart. 'How did you come to hear about it?'

'The police aren't totally inactive in the matter of these kidnappings,' Laker said. 'I have people keeping watch, certain villains are under my eye, as you might say. One of my men happened to be nearby at the time.'

'What? Then why didn't he help?'

Laker looked uncomfortable. 'That was regrettable, but I don't think he was at fault. Having observed Mr Simon Roper following a rogue that any sensible young gentleman would avoid, my sergeant decided to keep an eye on him. He couldn't intervene at that point without jeopardizing his own position. Unfortunately he lost sight of both men somewhere in the vicinity of the Newscombe Street Mews, which left him much concerned, but unsure what action he might take. However, more than three hours later, much to his relief, he saw Mr Roper again. The young man emerged, somewhat the worse

144

for wear, and in the company of a local doctor, from the house of Sir Mortimer Bantry, in Lucas Place. I am hoping you may be able to enlighten me as to what happened in the meantime.'

'I'll tell you what I know,' Jocelyn said. 'I asked my nephew to join us this morning, as he could give you a more detailed account than I, but regrettably he has absented himself. I fear he is out working on the case again.'

'Oh?' The policeman hunched forward in his chair. 'So you don't know where he is? That's not good news, Mr Roper. With all due respect, your nephew is making himself altogether too visible, and it's most unwise of him.'

'I agree.' Jocelyn sighed. 'My nephew has been in my care for many years, Inspector, and he has rarely been wayward, but in this instance he has defied me.'

Laker shook his head. 'Young men are all too ready to throw over the traces these days. I don't know where they learn such disrespect. Let's hope he'll be sensible and return home soon. You'll have heard a little about this man Mudd; he's a great deal cleverer than he looks. We know his employer operates somewhere near the mews, but we've not been able to pinpoint his lair. Rogues who are usually willing to sell their souls for a few shillings are terrified of Mudd, and nobody has even got a clear look at the villain who pays his wages. He's a master at keeping out of sight; so far my sergeant has only caught a glimpse of him once, and didn't see enough to be sure of knowing him again. I confess I was hoping Mr Simon Roper would be able to help us.

What he saw the other night could make the first solid evidence for our case.'

'I'm afraid even if he was here, he couldn't be much help to you.' Jocelyn related what he knew of Simon's capture and escape, and went on to explain about his nephew's amnesia. 'I think that's why he refused to stay home; he has a perverse hope that he might encounter this man again, and that the meeting will jog his memory. It doesn't seem to occur to him that Mudd might take the opportunity to finish what was attempted the other night.'

'So,' Inspector Laker said, 'there are underground tunnels joining one side of Lucas Place to Newscombe Street. I should have made the connection; the sergeant suspected there might be cellars under the mews. A bit of gambling goes on amongst the grooms and drivers now and then, and evidently when he was in uniform, years ago, he chased a couple of villains into what should have been a dead end, but they vanished. They must have known about these secret passages, and dived into them when they heard him coming for them. And no wonder Mudd can vanish so quickly, he and his master could be using any one of half-a-dozen different houses.'

'This probably doesn't bring you any nearer to making an arrest,' Jocelyn said.

'Maybe not, but we've got two witnesses who could well put Mudd behind bars. There's a little scheme they've been working for months, but of late they've become careless. When they aren't kidnapping children, Mudd and his master are providing new blood for some of the higher class

146

brothels in the city. It's a neat trick. In some big mansion you'll find a servant in their pay, and that servant arranges for a new young housemaid to be dismissed, before she's had time to make friends with the other staff and settle in properly. Then he or she pretends to be sympathetic, tells the girl how unfair it is, being turned off without a character, and tells her where she can find a kind woman who'll give her another job.'

'But that position is found to be in a brothel,' Jocelyn said. 'Yes, I've heard of something similar, from Mrs Marchant.'

'For the first week or two the girl's treated well enough, though she's kept below stairs and given no chance to get away. Gradually she realizes she's in a whorehouse, but by then she's being indoctrinated by the madam and the other girls, given new clothes, petted and flattered, and told she's worth something better than scrubbing floors. In a week or two she's either persuaded or forced into entertaining the clients.'

'And you can link this to the man who imprisoned and threatened my nephew?' Jocelyn asked.

'We hope to, very soon,' the inspector said. 'Two of the girls managed to escape, and they're ready to lay a complaint. We'll get Mudd at least.'

'But he's only the brawn, you need to find the brains as well. Now that you know about the cellars, surely you'll take a closer look at the residents of Lucas Place?'

'That seems the obvious next move,' Laker said. 'I'm afraid my sergeant has been wasting his time on Choker, the man who runs the mews; I confess I rather fancied him as our prime suspect too, but thanks to an accident he suffered as a child, his voice sounds like handfuls of gravel rattling in a barrel, and he's no gentleman.'

'I have started discreet enquiries about numbers three and four Lucas Place,' Jocelyn said, taking two sheets of paper from a drawer. 'If what little information I have gleaned so far is of use to you, then you are very welcome to it.'

'Thank you.' Laker sounded despondent. He scanned the pages briefly, nodding. 'A start at least. We'll eliminate Choker, and start again from scratch. It would be useful to speak to Miss Bantry, but it would be best if her involvement was kept quiet, so we'll let that pass for now. Perhaps we'll find some way after we've made the arrests. There's a good chance that, unlike your nephew, she can identify Mudd's employer; she sounds a most courageous young woman, but we mustn't risk drawing attention to her.'

'Indeed. I shall be eternally grateful to her,' Jocelyn said. 'It took great presence of mind to act as she did, but it was hardly what's expected of a respectable young woman, and we must also think of her reputation. Inspector, I shan't deny that I am worried about my nephew's safety; do you think that concern is justified? Am I exaggerating the risk?'

Laker looked at him, a mute sympathy in his expression. He slowly shook his head. 'We think Mudd knows that his prisoner didn't drown,' he said sombrely. 'There's a rumour that's being repeated too often to be untrue. Mudd is offering a reward for information. He's said to be looking for a tall young gentleman with his arm in a sling.'

In the uncertain pre-dawn light, a massive figure emerged from the deep shadows surrounding Newscombe Street mews. Making little sound for such a large man, he crossed the stableyard and trod softly up an outside staircase, knocking once on the door at the top.

'What!' A hoarse voice croaked from inside. The door opened. 'Cuss it, Mudd, what time d'yer call this?'

'If it's a time you ain't interested in makin' money, Choker,' came the muttered reply, as Mudd pushed his way into the room, 'I'll eat me bleedin' 'at.'

Down below, a heap of sacks lying beside the dung heap stirred. A tall, thin shape rose from beneath the filthy burlap, stretching warily. Shivering in the chill as he moved away from the heap's warmth, the man padded across the cobbles to the place where Mudd had materialized, peering into the dark, feeling around wooden panels and crumbling brick walls.

Two minutes passed, then the door at the top of the stairs opened quietly, and Mudd descended. At the bottom he hesitated for a second, before striding towards the street entrance. By the gate his boot caught on something and he lurched, almost falling. 'Gawd!'

The tall man uncurled and tried to rise, but Mudd was surprisingly quick, and a huge hand clamped tight around his ankle and jerked him back to the ground.

''Oo's this? Oh, it's you, is it?' Mudd stared into

the man's face, but he didn't let him go. 'Can't you find no better place to kip?'

'Choker threw me out. You got any more errands you want run?'

'I dunno, maybe. You was told to spread the word, but 'ow do I know where you've bin an' 'oo you've told? I want the 'ole bloomin' city to know I'm lookin' for a young bleeder wiv a damaged left paw.'

'I did what you said.' The man nodded up at him. 'Over the river, the docks, everywhere, just like you told me. And about there being money in it once you get him.'

Mudd made a sound of disbelief. 'Yeah, well, I ain't 'ad no takers yet, so I ain't payin', see? An' that goes for you an' all.' Relinquishing his hold on his victim's arm, he transformed his meaty hand into a fist and aimed a powerful punch at the man's head.

There wasn't time to dodge, and the blow slammed him into the gatepost; for a second the deep blue of the sky turned to black, and when the tall man recovered enough to look for Mudd, the one-time pugilist was already turning the corner into Lucas Place, whistling merrily, as if this unnecessary act of violence had cheered him.

Slowly, massaging his skull, Mudd's victim rose to his feet. As he straightened, throwing back his shoulders, he seemed to grow in stature; his silhouette in the gloom looked every inch the old soldier. For a moment he stood irresolute. There was nobody to see him, but from within the stables came a muffled curse, then the patter of feet, and this seemed to help him make up his mind.

150

Taking a battered and ragged hat from his pocket, the man slammed it on his head. He thrust his hands into his pockets and slumped, his military bearing gone. Slouching, head down, he went after Mudd.

Simon Roper hunched his shoulders, pulling the thin old coat he was wearing tighter around him against the early morning air. The previous evening had been wasted; he had roamed the crowded streets, mingling with the smartly dressed crowds going to theatres and clubs, fearful of venturing where Mudd or his cronies might spot him, knowing he was being prudent, yet angry at himself for his cowardice.

Once he could be sure his uncle had retired for the night he had returned to the house, but he hadn't slept much; now, dressed little better than a tramp and with his injured hand thrust into a deep pocket, he felt almost invisible. Men and women hurrying to work, emerging from doors, scurrying up basement steps to blink in the growing light, paid him no attention as he plodded slowly along in the gutter, a woollen scarf, unravelling at the ends, pulled up high around neck and chin, and a hat drooping over his eyes. Even so, he wouldn't risk his disguise anywhere near Lucas Place or Newscombe Street.

If he couldn't go looking for Mudd, there was still Higgs. After their encounter the previous day, Simon was sure the man could be a useful source of information, but he thought his uncle had made a mistake in approaching him out in the open. He had seen naked greed awakened in

Higgs's eyes at the sight of gold; offer him enough when he was away from prying eyes, and he had to succumb to temptation.

Simon had wrapped ten guineas in a small leather pouch, and bound it tightly against his splinted fingers before tying a dirty rag over the whole thing. It made his battered hand feel very heavy and uncomfortable, but he could think of no more secure place to carry the money; he doubted anyone would suspect it was there. Ten guineas was a large sum of money to a budding journalist, but it would be worth every penny if it led to the identity of the man who had threatened to have him thrown into a watery grave. Only when Mudd and his employer were both behind bars could he be sure that Virginia Bantry was truly safe.

Lowe Street opened up before him, a hive of almost respectable activity amidst the surrounding poverty. Higgs's barrow wasn't there. Simon wandered among the stalls, careful to keep his pace slow and deliberate, and his head down. As he passed the pot seller, the man gave him a sudden shove in the back. Simon fell, his injured hand jerking from his pocket as he tried to save himself, but it tangled in the torn old coat and didn't come free quickly enough to keep him from landing face down in a pile of unidentifiable filth. 'Clear orf,' a rough voice said. 'Ain't no pickin's 'ere fer your sort.'

Gagging at the stench, spitting to clear something slimy and unspeakably foul from his mouth, Simon heaved himself to his knees, fury coursing through him. Intent on retaliation, he curled his right hand into a fist, studying the pot seller from beneath the brim of his battered hat. The man was about his equal in height and maybe weighed a little more, but at school Simon had been renowned for his powerful right hook; he could put this opponent down with a single blow, and his injured left hand would be no handicap.

Two small boys hooted derisively as Simon hawked and spat and wiped a grimy sleeve across his face. One of them bent to pick up a rotten apple lying at his feet and, as he straightened, he caught sight of the rag that swathed Simon's left hand. Eyes widening, the child paused, looking puzzled. It was enough to bring Simon back to his senses. Silently, cursing inwardly, he thrust the tell-tale bandage back out of sight; he couldn't afford to arouse curiosity. He unclenched his fist, turning from the boys and cramming his hat more firmly down on his head. The stallholder sent a swift kick after him as he lurched away.

Finding a refuge in a bricked-up doorway, Simon sank down and wrapped himself in his coat, intent on escaping notice until Higgs appeared. Time passed slowly; he grew thirsty and looked with longing at the drinking fountain on the other side of the street; a gift to the market from some long-forgotten benefactor, it was always surrounded by urchins and chattering women and he had no wish to attract any more attention to himself.

The stream of life passed by, and Simon fell into a doze. Jolting from sleep, he saw that Higgs had arrived, but he made no move, watching as the man sold some of his goods and exchanged curses with his neighbour. After a while Higgs beckoned to one of the urchins by the fountain; when the boy came he spoke briefly before cuffing him round the ear. Evidently the child was being charged with minding the barrow. Fully awake and alert now, Simon began to ease into movement. By the time Higgs strode away, weaving between the market-traders to cross the street, he was on his feet and ready to follow.

Higgs never looked back, walking at a leisurely pace, so it was easy to keep him in sight without getting too close. His route led Simon out of the narrow back streets, down a busy road filled with traffic, until suddenly they were leaving all the hustle and bustle behind; there were no more cabs or omnibuses, only ragged men and women and an occasional barrow. As the way grew ever narrower and darker, so the people looked dirtier and more shrunken, until even in his disguise Simon felt out of place. He thought he could feel eyes watching from the small blank windows on either side. A woman stepped from the shadows, her gaunt face pale.

'Lookin' for me, 'andsome?'

'Got no money,' Simon growled, keeping his head turned away from her. She spat and vanished, back into whatever den she had crawled from.

Glancing uneasily behind him, Simon saw no reason to worry, but he walked on with caution, ears and eyes stretched; he had no wish to turn from hunter to prey. Higgs was maybe thirty yards ahead; still without looking to left or right, the man swivelled on his heel and entered a pot-house, where a dingy sign above the door swung to and fro, the image upon it too worn to be recognizable. Shuffling a little nearer, Simon found himself by a closed door with dirt heaped in front of it. It looked as if nobody had passed that way in years, so he sank back against the damp wood; with luck he would be invisible here, as he had at the market, and be ignored as just one more piece of human flotsam.

The coins felt heavy, the weight dragging uncomfortably against his injured hand; he wished he had brought some small copper coins, to buy food and drink, but perhaps it was for the best that he had not. While he might look like a vagrant, he doubted his ability to sound sufficiently like one to convince the local people.

When the door was dragged swiftly inwards, Simon tipped back with it. He had a brief glimpse of dark cloth as something was tossed over his head, engulfing him.

'Quick.' It was the only word he heard, but he knew Higgs's voice and realized with sickening certainty that the man had outsmarted him, had probably led him quite deliberately to this spot. Four strong hands held Simon down, capturing his arms; there was no chance of making any sort of resistance, folded as he was in the smothering cloth. A rope was passed around his body and pulled tight, and he was dragged through the doorway. With a squeal of hinges and the grind of protesting wood, the door closed.

Chapter Fourteen

In the nightmare moment after he fell backwards through the doorway, Simon thought Higgs planned to choke him to death. He lashed out, close to panic, accidentally slamming his injured hand into something hard and unyielding. Pain made the world spin and he felt himself falling down a black spiral into unconsciousness. When he returned to his senses a little later the terror had passed; he was swathed in thick suffocating cloth and tightly bound, but he was very much alive.

'Ain't dead, is 'e?' said a querulous voice.

'Not yet,' Higgs replied, 'but I wouldn' give much fer 'is chances once Mudd comes fer 'im. Come on, we'll stow 'im in 'ere, while I sends a message.'

Simon was lifted, carried a short way and dropped none too lightly to the floor. Another door slammed shut, and two sets of footsteps thudded their way across creaking floorboards, before fading away. There were sounds from somewhere far below; he was above the gin shop.

Thirst soon became a problem. Simon had been unpleasantly dry when he sat watching for Higgs; that mild discomfort seemed a mere nothing now. Dust from the sacking that covered his head was clogging his throat, and his tongue felt too big for his mouth. He had no idea how much time had passed, but by now his uncle would have met the police inspector; Jocelyn Roper would be angry, thinking Simon's absence was another act of defiance. A small moan escaped him as cramp seized the muscles in his legs, but he was too closely wrapped to do anything to assuage it. The packet of sovereigns lay beneath him, and they were pressing painfully into his broken fingers; it felt as if the splints had moved. Somehow he doubted if that would matter soon; he was surprised to have survived so long. Perhaps Higgs hadn't been able to locate Mudd. Simon bit hard on his lip. He was a prisoner, lashed in a tight cocoon from head to ankles, but as long as he took slow deep breaths, air continued to filter through the folds of fabric. Fear wouldn't get the better of him again; a man might be helpless, yet still retain his dignity.

There didn't seem any likelihood of escape or rescue; he couldn't expect the kind of luck that had brought Virginia to him to occur a second time. Why the thought hadn't come to him sooner he couldn't say, but suddenly it was there, echoing around his skull as if somebody had shouted in his ear. He had forgotten about Virginia! Her situation was every bit as perilous as his. Obviously he had been captured on Mudd's orders, or rather on the orders of Mudd's mysterious master; they must have known all along that he hadn't drowned, and by now they must have worked out how he had been rescued. By meeting Virginia in the park near Lucas Place, he had as good as led them directly to her.

Close to panicking again, Simon told himself

that Virginia should be safe during the day; Mrs Kington never let her leave the house without company, and even Mudd wouldn't try anything in broad daylight. Which left the night – he had begged her not to go near the cellars, but she had refused to give him her promise. What would she think when he didn't turn up for their rendezvous? Would his uncle go in his place, as he had suggested he might?

He had to escape. Determined to disguise himself properly this time, and aware that his previous costume had been sadly amateurish, Simon was carrying nothing that would be out of place in a tramp's possession, apart from the hidden coins. However, there was a small broken penknife in his pocket, an old treasure from his childhood; the blade was less than an inch long, and only a vagrant with nothing better would have bothered to pick up such a thing. Simon had dismissed all hope of using it, since it nestled snugly in his pocket, impossible to reach. However, his hands weren't actually bound; he had been bundled up like a parcel, rolled in the filthy sacking and encircled by many loops of rope, so his arms were lashed against his body.

By breathing in deeply, tensing his muscles and then releasing them, he managed to move his right hand half an inch; if he could go on doing that, eventually he might reach his pocket.

'Imagine what Sir Mortimer will say,' Mrs Yelding chirped, putting her arm through Virginia's as they walked through the park gates, 'to find you so fortunate in your neighbours. You haven't met

158

young Mr Parkin yet, of course, but he lives so near, and is so eager to meet Sir Mortimer because of his interest in Roman archaeology, that I am sure it won't be long before you are introduced. I confess he doesn't have quite the handsome looks of Reverend Solcott or the charm of Mr Roper, but he is quite eligible. I asked him about the work that has been done at the back of the house, and he told me he is having the stables improved. He intends keeping a carriage, as well as a riding horse.'

'Doesn't he have a carriage already?' Virginia asked. 'I thought I'd seen one turning in beyond the major's house.'

'That was more likely to be Reverend Solcott's, although I would expect you to be familiar with that particular carriage, since you travelled home from church in it on Sunday.'

'I saw a different one. Perhaps it belonged to a visitor.'

'Oh, I do hope so. I always enjoy it when people come to Lucas Place, it is so exciting to make new acquaintances.' Mrs Yelding glanced at Virginia. 'Perhaps having three young gentlemen competing for your attention isn't enough for you,' she added mischievously.

'I'd hardly count Mr Parkin, since I haven't even met him. And Mr Solcott isn't exactly young,' Virginia protested, 'he must be well over thirty years old.'

'Thirty-five is the perfect age for a man to marry! I only hope I am included when your cousin invites his new neighbours to dine, to see how this rivalry sharpens your suitors' wits. I have no doubt you will be cruel to them.'

Virginia laughed. 'That's a ridiculous accusation, and you know it.'

Mrs Yelding gave an exaggerated sigh. 'All that power. I can barely remember how it felt.'

'It's not a power I want, thank you.' A faint flush rose to Virginia's cheeks. 'It's you who are cruel, teasing me like this. And I think you already know there's only one man I want my cousin to be pleased with.'

'Maybe. But you are still young, and girls can change their minds. You may find your affections settle upon Mr Parkin instead.'

'It's a shame he didn't come to our door and ask for an invitation to the cellars,' Virginia quipped, forgetting for a moment that this was the man she suspected of being a kidnapper, and quite possibly a murderer. 'That would have been the ideal opportunity for us to get acquainted, alone in the dark. Roman ruins are very romantic.'

Mrs Yelding giggled. 'Really, my dear, such a suggestion. However, I'm sure he intends to ask Sir Mortimer for permission to explore beneath your house, as soon as he can.' She looked around the park. 'I see no sign of Mr Roper, I had expected him to be waiting by the pond. Perhaps we should sit down for a moment and wait.'

The day was threatening rain, and Virginia let her gaze roam idly over the few people who were out taking the air. She paused, a little frown between her brows, as she noticed the bent old man staring into the water on the other side of the lake. It was the idler who had been there the previous day, the one Simon thought looked like the tall, soldierly man who might be involved with Mudd; now she looked more closely she could see what he meant. The loiterer was younger than his bent back suggested, and she had the disconcerting feeling that he had been watching her until she turned to look his way.

'Miss Bantry.' Virginia looked up quickly, startled to find her gaze met by a pair of familiar blue eyes.

'Mr Roper.' She looked around quickly in the hope that Simon had accompanied his uncle, trying to hide her disappointment when she realized the older man had come alone. 'This is a pleasant surprise.'

'The pleasure is mine. I am here with an apology. My nephew finds himself unable to meet you today.'

As she introduced the newspaper proprietor to her neighbour, Virginia noted that he looked tired; there were new lines around his eyes, and his complexion looked much paler than on their previous meetings. However, he cheerfully offered Virginia and Mrs Yelding an arm each, expressing his willingness to escort them around the lake.

Mrs Yelding declined. 'I believe you will be quicker without me,' she said. 'I shall be quite comfortable sitting here. You shouldn't linger, for it looks as if it may come on to rain.'

'I am so glad you have come,' Virginia said, as soon as they were out of earshot. 'I have news about Lucas Place. Mr Jeffrey Parkin has returned to number three, next to Mrs Yelding and her sister, and something has happened that makes him an obvious suspect. He called on them this morning, asking to be allowed to visit their cellar. He said he had an interest in archaeology and wanted to inspect the Roman vaults that he believed were under their house. I think that is merely a ruse, and he hopes to find out how your nephew escaped from his imprisonment.'

'Miss Bantry, I must ask you not to concern yourself any further with this affair.' Jocelyn Roper looked grave. 'It is good of you to try to assist us, and I shall pass this information to the police, but please, dismiss the whole matter from your mind.'

'Is nothing to be done about the child I saw in the carriage?' Virginia asked, ignoring his plea. 'Perhaps that is why Mr Simon Roper couldn't come?'

'Inspector Laker of the detective division was with me earlier today, and I am assured that his men have the case in hand. As for my nephew, he has been pursuing his own enquiries, but both he and the inspector have told me to warn you, most emphatically, not to venture into the cellars below Lucas Place again.'

'But what about that poor girl?' she persisted, making no effort to hide her anger. 'Nobody is trying to help her. Each day that passes makes it more likely that she will be sent away to her fate, and she may never be found. Who knows, perhaps she is about to be taken out of reach even as we speak.'

'I understand your concern, but her existence is little more than conjecture, there could be some other explanation for what you saw. Inspector Laker's men will bring these villains to justice, and you could jeopardize more than your own welfare if you interfere. For your own sake, Simon won't see you again until this case is closed. He will not risk bringing you to the attention of such men as Mudd and his master. Please, stay away from the cellar, and make sure the door that gives access to it is kept securely locked.'

There seemed to be no way to reply to such a demand, and Virginia swallowed her protests. Taking leave of Mr Roper, she accompanied Mrs Yelding out of the park. Mr Roper had spoken optimistically of an end to the affair, and assured her she had jumped to conclusions about the child, but she knew what she had seen. Captive, terrified, the girl had nevertheless tried to attract somebody's attention. Virginia was consumed by a helpless anger; if she was a man she would be looking for the other end of the passageway, where Willshire had stepped out into daylight, but a young woman could hardly loiter around the mews.

'Oh look, here comes Mr Parkin.' Mrs Yelding gave Virginia's arm a squeeze. 'You can't tell me you aren't curious to meet him, for you were eager enough with your questions when I told you he was home.'

An undersized young man with a narrow face and very thin arms and legs was coming towards them. Even before he opened his mouth to return Mrs Yelding's greeting, Virginia knew she had been wrong; this young man might be clever, and possibly he knew a great deal about archaeology, but he wasn't Mudd's master. She hadn't seen the man in the cellar clearly, but he was both taller and broader than Mr Parkin. The first few words he spoke confirmed her opinion: Jeffrey Parkin's voice was as thin and reedy as his body.

As she made polite conversation, Virginia's thoughts were far away; eliminating Mr Parkin from her list left only one possible suspect amongst those living in Lucas Place: the kidnapper had to be Reverend Solcott's mysterious brother.

Her attention had wandered, but suddenly something Mr Parkin said made Virginia's eyes open wide. 'You say you called at Major Brand's house?' she repeated.

'Indeed, but I heartily wished I had not. With their master away it seems the servants act as they please. I was treated with abominable rudeness and the words they used to me aren't fit to repeat in decent company. Considering the major's tenant is a clergyman, he keeps a most unruly household. I have heard the most disturbing sounds from the attic rooms, somebody crying and moaning, at all hours. It woke me before dawn this morning.'

'I expect it is nothing more than a homesick maid,' Mrs Yelding said reassuringly.

'But there could be a more sinister reason,' Virginia said. 'Reverend Solcott mentioned his brother to me, and I suspect he is the black sheep of the family. We know he comes to stay at the house now and then. Who knows what such a man might get up to when his brother is away.'

'Really Virginia, how can you say such things?' Mrs Yelding protested. 'You have been reading too many novels. As for Reverend Solcott's brother, I

164

know of nobody who has even met him.'

'I have no wish to meet him,' Jeffrey Parkin said, 'nor the master of the house, unless he can keep his servants in check.' He bowed briefly to Virginia. 'My hopes of gaining entrance to the Roman cellars now lie in Sir Mortimer Bantry's hands; perhaps you will be kind enough to present my compliments to him, and tell him I shall wait on him very soon.'

'Of course,' Virginia said, 'and I hope when you come, you will be able to tell us all about our mysterious underground labyrinth.'

And before that, she thought defiantly, since nobody else is prepared to take action, I shall do some more exploring of my own.

Chapter Fifteen

The thin blade ripped into the cloth. Simon felt cool air upon his hand and saw the meagre light that spilled into his prison. His fingers were slippery with blood, for he had made many false attempts, and the knife seemed more inclined to cut into his hand than through the tough fibres, but he had the sharp edge hard against the rope now, and could sense the cords yielding to the bite of the steel. Working with new hope, and with a frantic energy fuelled by fear for Virginia, he felt the first strands part; his captors had left him alone for a long time, and he must be free and gone from this place before they returned.

165

The sounds of revelry from below had grown. It sounded as if a dozen men and women were alternately squabbling and laughing uproariously, the din they made punctuated by the occasional pounding of feet on rickety stairs, which set Simon's heart pounding in its turn, lest it should be Higgs, returning at last with Mudd.

He was hot and breathless by the time the rope finally gave way, but once it parted his arm had more room to move, and the second rope was easier. In another minute he was able to push the sacking away from his face, and he gratefully gulped air into his lungs. Freeing his head from his cocoon, he strained to see the knots that secured him, but the darkness was creeping further into the dingy room; he groped urgently with a bloody hand, and began to saw at another rope.

In the gin shop a near riot seemed to have erupted; at least he needn't be afraid that his escape attempts would be heard. Even as this thought occurred to him, voices from close by made him pause.

'What now?' It was the querulous man who had helped Higgs capture him.

'We'll 'ave to wait. Mudd's off somewhere, an' 'is lordship won't deal wiv the likes of you an' me, not now 'e's so 'igh an' mighty. Take a gander at our prize, make sure 'e's still tucked up comfy like.'

Simon had only a second. He grabbed at the loose rope and pulled it, before rolling over to hide the ripped sacking that had exposed his head. Lying still, he tried to keep his breathing slow and shallow. A door opened briefly, and snapped shut.

'Right 'n' tight. You sure Mudd's good fer that

twenty guineas?'

'It ain't Mudd, it's 'is boss, an' 'e'll pay right enough. Come a long way, 'e 'as, since 'e was a swell mobsman, workin' Drury Lane.'

'What? You know 'im? I 'eard nobody ever sees 'im, an' Mudd keeps 'is trap shut an' all.'

'Ain't many knows what I know.' Higgs sounded complacent.

'I 'eard 'e's a proper gent. There's even some say 'e wears a dog collar.'

'Dresses like a crow, don't 'e, but 'e was plain Sol Crick when I knew 'im. Come on, I fancy a wet.'

Footsteps could be heard as the two men descended some stairs. Simon let out a long relieved breath then began to attack the ropes in a near-frenzy; what he had just overheard made it even more imperative that he escape, and quickly.

How he came to hear the creak of the rotting floorboard he didn't know; the noise was so unexpected that a dry gasp of alarm escaped his swollen throat. Frantically he tried to get his arm free; the tiny blade would be useless as a weapon, but he wouldn't submit to anyone without a fight.

'Quiet,' a voice ordered. 'Keep still and keep your mouth shut, and you might get out of here alive.' Simon felt hands grab hold of his feet through the sacking, and he was dragged swiftly across the floor.

'Let me go!' Simon croaked, still struggling to release his arm.

'Stow the noise, or you'll get us both killed,' the newcomer hissed. 'They could come back any minute.'

Simon felt himself thrown up across the man's

shoulders, his head hitting the door so hard that he saw lightning flash before his eyes. He was carried up a narrow stair, and for a few brief seconds, looking up past the man's straining shoulders, he could see the faint glow of stars far above. Another minute and they were out in the open air. Simon was suspended fifty feet above the tumble of buildings, staring dizzily down at a heart-stopping drop. Grunting with effort, his deliverer carried him along a ledge that skirted the roof, climbed a shallow slope, slid down another, and came to rest in a lead-lined gully. Here he dropped Simon, none too gently, then went scurrying back the way they had come, a tall, lanky figure who stretched his length on the slates to stare down, his head cocked as if he was listening.

'Who are you?' Simon demanded.

'Hush!' An arm waved at him impatiently. The man remained where he was, gazing at the alley far below, his head turned away so his face couldn't be seen.

Gathering his scattered wits, Simon renewed his efforts with the tiny steel blade; his shoulder had come free during the breakneck escape, and it was easier now to reach the ropes. There were shouts from below, a furious bellow rising over the general hubbub of the night-time city.

'Somebody must have seen us,' his rescuer whispered. 'Quiet now, and keep still, or we're both dead men.' It sounded as if the place they had just left was being torn apart. Wood splintered and glass shattered. After a brief lull, Simon heard footsteps crashing in stairways, then screams and cries of protest, but the sounds were receding; the hunt was going away from them.

On the roof there was silence for several long, breathless minutes. Simon was struggling to sit up when his rescuer slid back down the slates to join him. With a few quick slashes from a sharp knife, he removed the rest of the ropes.

'Who are you?' Simon asked again, thrusting the bloody little blade back into his pocket.

The man didn't answer, pointing instead. 'We go that way.' He turned his back and walked along the gully, an upright figure against the stars. Every muscle in Simon's body seemed to have stiffened into cramps, but he crawled after the stranger as best he could, finally managing to get to his feet. They went by a devious route around chimneys and across perilously ruinous rooftops, finally descending by a series of rickety wooden ladders within a block of ramshackle dwellings. Ill-wrapped bodies stirred in their slumbers and cursed them sleepily as they passed.

Stumbling into a yard that stank like a midden, Simon almost fell against a pump. Disregarding any risk, he grasped the handle and pumped vigorously, putting his head beneath the flow of water, reviving as he gulped some of it down his parched throat, revelling in its coldness as it soaked his face and hair. When he looked up the man who had led him to freedom was twenty yards away and moving fast, as if intent on leaving him behind.

'No, wait,' Simon rasped. The figure was suddenly familiar. 'I know you.' He stumbled after his deliverer, grabbing his shoulder and pulling him round. He'd first seen that face in Lucas Place. This man had held the doctor's horse; he'd

169

witnessed Simon's meeting with Virginia Bantry in the park, and vanished when Simon tried to follow him from Lowe Street.

'I'm Sergeant Beddowes of the detective division,' the man replied, freeing himself from Simon's grip. 'You'll excuse me, sir, I've work to do.'

'A detective!' Simon stared at him in wonder. 'I suppose that explains a great deal. At least let me thank you.'

'There's no need, I was just doing my job.' Beddowes pointed. 'Go that way, take the first right, and you'll find yourself on familiar ground. If you've any sense, Mr Roper, you'll go home and stay there.'

'Not until I tell you what I heard from Higgs,' Simon said. 'I think it might be of use to you. I know the name of Mudd's master, and a good deal more besides.'

Jocelyn paced the floor, pausing to look down into the street for the tenth time. There was still copy to be written for the next edition of the *Examiner;* an uncompleted article lay on his desk, but when he sat down and tried to read the sentences he had constructed with such care the day before, they made no sense. He turned to look at the clock; the hands both pointed to twelve, but his mind was far away, and the time didn't register at first. When it did, a kind of shudder passed through him; Simon had been gone for seventeen hours, and he couldn't get Laker's warning out of his head.

As if the man had been summoned by the

thought, his next visit to the window showed the police inspector climbing out of a hansom cab and hurrying across the pavement. Jocelyn, abandoning his usual ponderous gait, went running down the stairs to let him in.

'I didn't expect to see you so soon, Inspector,' Jocelyn said, ushering the man upstairs.

'I have news,' Laker said. 'I thought I should speak to you and your nephew as soon as possible. He's here, I take it?'

'No, he's still not home.' Jocelyn slumped behind his desk, too agitated to think of offering his guest the tobacco jar.

'Not home!' Laker had been lowering himself into a chair, but he straightened again, staring at the editor as if he couldn't believe what he was hearing. 'Then where has he gone? This young man defies all sense, Mr Roper. Beddowes left him barely an hour ago, having rescued him from a most perilous situation, at some considerable risk to himself. He watched him until he was clear of the stews to the east of Lowe Street market, and was assured that he was on his way home.'

'Lowe Street? Just an hour ago? We paid a visit there together, but I can think of no reason for him to go again. And who is Beddowes?'

'My best detective. Sergeant Beddowes had been watching the area around Newscombe Mews.' The policeman shook his head. 'This is a worrying turn of events. Thanks in some part to your nephew, we may soon be in a position to make an arrest, but I'd be happier to have him safely out of the way at present.'

There was a discreet tap at the street door, and

171

Laker started. 'That will be Beddowes now, I told him to meet me here. With your permission, I shall bring him in, I think he ought to know that young Mr Roper didn't come home.' Jocelyn Roper nodded and Laker left, hurrying back down the stairs, to return a minute later, followed by the sergeant.

Beddowes was tall, and stood very upright, but in all other ways he was unremarkable; he was clean-shaven with brown hair greying at the temples. His clothes were shabby, his boots well-worn but reasonably clean. He might have been a minor tradesman, just scraping a living; nobody encountering him in the street would have given him a second look, except perhaps to remark on his military bearing.

'I'm sorry to hear young Mr Roper chose to ignore my advice, sir,' Beddowes said, once he'd been introduced to the newspaperman. 'Where do you think he's gone?'

'I know he was worried about the safety of Miss Virginia Bantry. Indeed, I share his concern. When I spoke to her earlier, and warned her to stay away from the cellars beneath Lucas Place, I had the feeling that she was most unwilling to obey.'

Beddowes shook his head, glancing at the inspector. 'It would be a bad thing if she ventured down there tonight, that's for sure.'

'We are on the verge of making some arrests,' Laker said. 'Perhaps I should explain. We had our doubts about one of the residents of Lucas Place, and dug up some rather interesting information; I was trying to work out how best to proceed when along comes your nephew and tells the

172

sergeant here something that really set the cat among the pigeons. I understand you had a visit from a well-known politician one night last week. He came here for the express purpose of dissuading you from publishing any more articles about the abduction of small children.'

'How did you know about that?' Roper's eyebrows rose. 'The meeting was supposed to be a secret.'

Laker laid a finger alongside his nose. 'We have our ways. The point is, that gentleman turns out to be closely related to the Reverend Gerard Solcott, and all our evidence points to that gentleman being the criminal we've been trying to track down.'

'Solcott? The man who lives in Lucas Place? I suppose I shouldn't be surprised, but the man's a cleric. Unless it's his brother–'

'There is no brother,' the inspector said. 'In fact, there is no Gerard Solcott, not any longer. The man at Lucas Place is an imposter. Gerard Solcott died of pneumonia, four years ago, shortly after taking the cloth.'

'What?' Jocelyn stared at him. 'But I heard his sermon at St Joseph's on Sunday!'

'The man using his name is a most accomplished villain by all accounts, quite an actor; he seems to have fooled the entire neighbourhood,' Laker said. 'According to what your nephew learnt from Higgs, his real name is Crick, and he's no more a clergyman than I am.'

'But this connection with a minister in Her Majesty's Government,' Jocelyn objected, 'if his relative is dead, why would he assist in this villain's deception?'

'For one very simple reason,' Laker replied bleakly. 'This man supplies something he wants, and no questions asked. By a stroke of extreme good fortune, I was able to ascertain that this eminent gentleman has, in the past, been suspected of debauching young girls, but thanks to his eminent position he managed to cover up the ensuing scandal. I knew I had no hope of arresting him, but I let it be known that he'd been discovered, and he has fled the country. Two of his servants, left in the lurch so to speak, are likely to tell us all we need to know, including how he came to use Solcott as a procurer.'

'Then what are you waiting for?' Jocelyn demanded. 'Why aren't you at Lucas Place, putting the villains under arrest?'

'Because both the phoney Solcott and his man, Mudd, have been away from Town. Mudd has returned, but we are still uncertain as to his employer's whereabouts. If we move too soon we might miss Crick, and I don't want that. As soon as he returns we shall be ready; with luck we'll be knocking at his door in the morning.'

'But what of Simon?' Jocelyn rose too. 'He could have gone there, thinking that Miss Bantry is in danger. Suppose he attempts to break in, or finds his way into the cellars?'

'Don't worry, sir,' Beddowes said. 'I'm going back there directly, to keep the place under observation. If I see any sign of your nephew I'll send him home, and this time I'll be sure to give him an escort; he'll not roam off again.'

Jocelyn stood staring at the door long after it

174

had closed behind the two policemen. He picked up his pipe and put it down again. With a weary sigh he pulled the unfinished article towards him.

The long day had come to an end, and Virginia was alone in her room at last, having dismissed Agnes as soon as she was free of her corset. There were still sounds from below stairs, but, according to Mr Willshire, all the preparations for Sir Mortimer's return would be completed very shortly, and the household could get a few hours of well-earned rest before the morning. She sat upon her bed, thinking about her cousin. His boat was expected to come in on the early morning tide, which meant he should be with them for a late breakfast. She couldn't help wondering what he would think of Simon; he couldn't object to her acquaintance, for Jocelyn Roper was already known to him, but she would be glad when their first meeting was over.

In reality that was the least of Virginia's worries; she didn't see any point in going to bed, for she doubted if she would sleep. She couldn't forget the meeting with Mr Parkin and his account of the child who cried in the night. It was impossible to let the matter rest there; as soon as the house was quiet she would creep downstairs and search the cellars, although from what their neighbour had said, it was more likely the child was being held in the attics. Even that would not deter her. If necessary she resolved to find a way into the house.

The clock in the hall struck, and Virginia counted to twelve; there had been no sound for some time. She reached for the plain dark dress she had left ready, then an idea struck her. Kneeling, she pulled a small trunk from beneath the bed. Under the few childhood belongings she had brought from India lay the clothes she had gathered with such care over the last few months, among them a shirt and pair of boots which had belonged to her cousin when he was a boy, and a pair of breeches bought from a tinker's cart. She had been unable to avoid Mrs Kington's presence during the transaction, but she had passed it off as a joke she intended to play on Sir Mortimer.

Virginia dressed quickly; she had practised many times, completing the costume by tucking her hair inside a cap, and putting on a loose jacket which hid her feminine curves. When she looked in the mirror she nodded approval; a fresh-faced youth of fourteen or fifteen years stared boldly back at her.

It was almost a commonplace now, to light the lamp she had fetched from the front parlour, and let herself in through the heavy door, with the spool of thread, her cousin's match box and a spare candle in her pocket. She was under no illusions; she could be running headlong into the most awful danger and her heart was thumping far too fast for comfort, but she was determined to go through with her mission.

Virginia had almost reached the broken door when a noise from behind brought her to a halt. With trembling fingers she turned the wick down until the flame died. She stood petrified in the darkness, scarcely breathing.

Chapter Sixteen

There were two distinct sets of footsteps, one quick and light, the other much heavier. Virginia shrank into a passage that led nowhere, to watch the approaching figures. Seeing the shadows wavering in the flickering lamplight, she was sure one of them was Willshire. The butler was using his own secret route to leave the house again, and taking somebody with him. His companion was small, and carried a bundle in one hand.

Greatly daring, Virginia moved quietly out of her hiding place once the two had passed by, and set off after them. She gaped as a beam from Willshire's lantern fell on the person at his side; it was Emily.

Why were they leaving the house in the middle of the night? Emily was terrified of the butler, and Virginia felt sure she wasn't going with him willingly.

'Please,' Emily said, her voice trembling a little, 'if I have to go, sir, I'd rather find my own place. And I shouldn't be wearing this, sir, I really shouldn't. I'll leave in the morning, I swear, if that's what you want.'

'What, in the middle of all the fuss and kerfuffle with our master expected home?' Willshire said. 'Don't be silly, girl. When the broken vases are discovered I shall have to tell Sir Mortimer how it happened. This way, at least you'll have a new position. As for the coat, Miss Bantry won't miss it, not with all the excitement tomorrow.'

'I feel all wrong about taking it,' the girl wailed. 'I know I left them pots near the edge of the table, but I don't know how they came to slide off that way.'

'You were careless,' Willshire barked. 'Quiet now. And hurry, we don't want to keep my friend waiting. You're to stay in his house overnight, and you'll be taken to your new place in the morning. Just consider yourself lucky: by rights I should have thrown you out without a character; think how that would have been, with nowhere to go but the streets.'

Virginia was shocked; had the butler deliberately made it look as if Emily had broken something? Everybody would assume that she had run away, and helped herself to her mistress's coat as she fled. In a flash Virginia recalled what Cook had said about the other kitchen girl who had left suddenly; had she too taken a midnight excursion with Willshire?

She must do something; she should call, demand that the man stop and explain himself, but the words stuck in her throat; she couldn't challenge him when she was dressed so outlandishly. Although appearing to defer to Mrs Kington in matters relating to Virginia, the butler had controlled the household since her cousin went away; they had both treated her as a child, with Willshire as much a figure of authority as her governess.

Before she could make up her mind what to do, the two ahead of her turned a corner. The light from the lantern vanished as if it had never been, and she was surrounded by total darkness. Too late, Virginia's courage reasserted itself; if her actions were condemned by Mrs Kington then she would have to appeal to her cousin for support.

Fumbling with the match box, she lit the lamp, but too much time had gone by. There was no sound from the passageway ahead. She ran, her steps echoing off the walls. 'Willshire,' she called, 'come back here at once. Where are you?'

There was no answer; they had gone. She bent low, searching for some sign of the scratches she had left when she and Emily had come this way before, but she could find none; she was in a large vaulted room where half a dozen tunnels vanished into blackness. Without some guide she dared go no further. Using the thread to explore would take hours, and she might still miss the way. Poor Emily. Was she to join the girl from the carriage? Perhaps Mr Parkin would be hearing the cries of two girls from the attics.

There had to be another way. Biting on her lip, Virginia returned to the more familiar part of the cellars, finding the crumbling door which would lead her to the place where she had found Simon. She almost ran through the gap; the door had been swung right back, but she was in too much of a hurry to notice, pausing only to lower the flame in the lamp so it barely showed a light. As she approached the hole in the wall, all appeared to be dark and silent, no sound issuing from the chamber where Simon had been held.

'Is anyone there?' Virginia whispered. Her voice echoed faintly back to her, and she could smell nothing but the stale still air. The bricks were piled precariously, and it appeared that some of them had fallen since she and Simon had left. Rashly she pushed at the remaining heap, and several more crashed to the ground on the other side of the wall. Virginia listened. The silence stretched into minutes and she dared to breathe again; with greater care she removed more of the bricks until the hole was wide enough to climb through.

Apart from the stone slab which had been dropped back over the noisome watercourse, nothing had changed since she was last here. Virginia tiptoed across the dusty floor, letting the light shine into each shadowy corner, reassuring herself that she was alone. It was a simple matter to find the steps leading up to the house, and within a minute she stood by a heavy wooden door.

When Simon arrived in Lucas Place there was a dim light showing in an upstairs room at Sir Mortimer Bantry's house, but now that window showed black. A warm glow shone briefly from the dingy little front parlour, the only room he remembered from his brief visit to the house; somebody had lit a lamp. He guessed that Virginia was there, in the room where, as far as he could recall, they had first met. Those few intimate moments had transformed him in some inexplicable way; since that meeting he found it hard to focus on anything but this amazing girl, who even now was probably putting herself into danger again. It was past midnight, he had heard the local clocks strike some time before, and he could think of only one reason why she should be there at such a late hour, when the rest of the

180

household were asleep.

The light dimmed, to reappear momentarily as a brightening of the glass above the front door. Simon climbed quickly from his hiding place on the basement steps of the empty house on the opposite side of the road; Virginia was going down to the cellars again. He ran to the front door and tapped on it gently, once, twice.

Surely she would hear him, surely she would feel his presence on the other side of the oak panels. He pressed his ear to the doorjamb. A sound came, muffled but recognizable; his heart sank. There was a thud and a click, as the cellar door was closed and locked. Simon lifted a hand to hammer at the door, then lowered it; if he raised the alarm in his current guise the servants would probably not even summon Mrs Kington. They would call the watchman, or hand him over to the police.

Keeping to the shadows and moving fast, Simon made his way to Newscombe Street. The mews was quiet apart from an occasional rustle as a horse shifted its weight. He crouched low, slithering noiselessly through an opening between the barn and the stables, watching the ground beneath his feet. Now, as never before, it was imperative that he find the entrance to the cellars.

Intent on his search, Simon almost missed the hint of movement, but a shift in the depth of shadow caught his eye, and he froze. A coach, leaning drunkenly on a broken wheel, stood behind the mews as if awaiting repair, Somebody had just climbed inside; there came the faint murmur of voices, a coarse laugh, and he saw the pale circle of a face at the window. A man was staring towards the backs of the houses in Lucas Place. Despite the poor light, Simon recognized him; it was Mudd. The man withdrew again, but Simon remained where he was; to move on he would have to cross open ground, and he would almost certainly be seen. At least while Mudd was here he wasn't in the cellars. Crouching down, Simon drew his old coat more tightly around him and settled down to wait, careful not to fidget in his impatience.

Time passed. A distant clock struck the half-hour. Simon's eyelids drooped, despite his fears for Virginia; it had been almost forty-eight hours since he had slept. The men in the carriage were quiet now, but Mudd poked his head out now and then, obviously expecting somebody to come. Simon too stared into the blackness, and was suddenly wide awake. A large bulky form was coming towards him, a gross, lopsided shape with a shaded lantern swinging from one hand. Simon gave an involuntary shiver, primeval fear eclipsing common sense, until he saw that the misshapen being was not one person, but two. A large, solidly built man was leading a smaller figure by the arm. This was a young woman, wrapped in a voluminous garment that covered her almost from head to foot; she seemed reluctant, as the man forced her to keep pace with him. Simon closed his hand into a fist; he'd reached the very heart of this wicked trade.

Mudd descended from the carriage, followed by a meagre man who padded silently in his wake. They went to meet the newcomers, and

182

when the girl recoiled he gave a low laugh. With practised ease he engulfed her in his arms, one hand covering her mouth as she gulped in air to scream. No more than a strangled cry escaped; anybody within earshot would think that the stable cat had caught a mouse.

'Show a glim,' Mudd ordered hoarsely, and the man who had brought the girl obediently opened the shutter on his lantern.

Simon had to bite down on his lip to prevent himself from calling out; the man holding the lamp was Willshire, butler to Sir Mortimer Bantry. He could see only the back of the girl's coat, and a few wisps of hair that had escaped from beneath the hood, but the small man's face was well lit; it was Choker, who ran the mews. Staring into the girl's face Choker nodded his approval, before drawing the butler aside, heading towards the spot where Simon was hiding.

Simon's heart was pounding so fast he thought it would burst; his attention was all for the figure being held so close by Mudd. He had seen that coat before; Virginia had worn it the night they met at Mr Cardew's house. All caution forgotten, he thrust to his feet, intent only on going to her.

All his thoughts on Virginia, Simon leapt forward. He didn't notice the old wheel half hidden by weeds at his feet, and he tripped, falling with his left hand beneath him. Pain sliced through him, a white hot agony, and he gasped. If they had heard him it would all have been over, for he was close to fainting. Trying to contain the spasms shooting up his arm, he came to his knees, watching through tear-filled eyes as Mudd lifted the girl

183

effortlessly across his shoulder, and hurried away.

'Well?' Willshire said, holding out a hand. 'You gave me your word.'

Choker responded with a sly smile. 'Until the next time, you're in the clear.' He dug in his pocket and pulled out a piece of paper, which he gave to the butler. 'You should be more careful where you make your wagers,' he said.

'I still say it was rigged,' Willshire growled back, snatching the paper and crumpling it in his hand. 'Maybe I'll find some other place to go.'

The small man shook his head. 'You're like the rest of them; gasping like a hooked fish!' With this jibe he melted into the shadows; Willshire stared after him for a moment then turned on his heel and marched away, the lantern swinging.

Virginia listened; there was no sound from inside the house. She would not go back, not until she had found out if Emily was imprisoned in the attics, like that other poor girl. If she was, then she must be rescued. Virginia spared a thought for Reverend Solcott; he was wrong to allow his brother to do as he pleased, so perhaps he must share a little of the blame, but it wouldn't occur to a decent man that a member of his family would take advantage of his kindness in such a terrible way.

The door was solid, but there was a small gap at the bottom. Bending down, she assured herself that no light shone through from the other side, which was encouraging. Virginia put down her lamp, reaching out to grasp the handle. Turning it very slowly, not daring to breathe, she was poised to run at the least sound from beyond the old oak panels. Well-oiled, the lock turned, and the door moved outwards beneath her hands. When it was open an inch she placed her eye to the gap, but all was dark.

Virginia was ready to push through the doorway, to race along the kitchen passage, where she could hope to find the entrance to the back stairs.

'Mudd, is that you?' The voice sounded very close.

'I'm 'ere, y'r honour,' came the reply, followed by footsteps on stone flags, growing gradually louder. Mudd was heading towards the very spot where she was hidden.

Brought abruptly to her senses, Virginia eased the door shut again, and gently released her hold on the handle. Mudd's footsteps passed by without stopping, and gradually the frantic beating of her heart steadied. She would have to wait for the household to settle to rest. Pulling the lamp to her she turned the wick very low. Virginia settled herself as comfortably as she could upon the top step, with her head against the door so she would hear if anyone came her way.

Time passed, and Virginia grew sleepy, despite the cold and the discomfort of the stone beneath her. There had been no sound from beyond the door, but she couldn't judge how long she had waited; it might be one o'clock, or even two; she felt as if she had sat there in the darkness for hours. She began to shiver, and knew it was as much from fear as from the chill of the air; if she didn't act soon, she might never have the courage to go on. She told herself that it was the cold

185

making her hands shake, as she eased the door open once more.

Reluctantly she abandoned the lamp; she still had the matchbox and a candle in her pocket, in case of need. Her first tentative steps took her into the kitchen, where a large clock ticked sombrely on the wall. Nothing stirred as she retreated; she had to find a way to the attics, but the back stairs would be unfamiliar to her; better to keep to areas she knew from her visits to the house as a guest of Mrs Brand.

The main staircase was thickly carpeted, and her feet made no sound as she trod softly up them and along the passage at the top. Finding the way to the next storey was simple too, for she had often been to the nursery occupied by the two younger Brand children.

A few minutes later, having safely negotiated the second floor, Virginia stood outside a plain door, the wood a little worn and cracked. This may be the way to another staircase, or simply another room. For the first time since she had entered the house, terror rose in her; one sound now, and she would run. She put a trembling hand on the latch, eased it up, and pulled the door. It opened with a loud protesting squeak.

'Well, well. What do we have here? A burglar? But a most unusual one.' Before her, a candlestick in his hand, stood a tall man, his head topped by a mop of fair hair. 'Come though. Is that a long curl I see escaping from under that cap?' He came closer, his features shifting disturbingly as the candle guttered in the sudden draught. With a gesture so quick she had no chance to stop him, he swept the cap from her head. 'I do believe it's Miss Bantry. This is a strange time to come visiting, my dear girl, and all unannounced.'

Chapter Seventeen

The man was laughing at her, white teeth gleaming in the sparse light. She couldn't see him clearly, but in shape and colouring he seemed a great deal like his brother.

'I love your costume, Miss Bantry, though it is a poor disguise, and rather an unwise one if you plan to go breaking into strangers' houses. You are far too pretty to be a boy, and I know of places where you'd be running a great risk appearing like that, far more so than if you were dressed in your most beautiful gown. My own tastes don't run that way; youths, no matter how handsome, are safe from me. I would prefer you to have come trespassing as a woman. Nevertheless I shall forgive your intrusion. I think that's quite magnanimous, don't you, considering this is the second time?'

'I beg your pardon,' Virginia said, putting every ounce of hauteur she could muster into her voice. 'I shall apologize to your brother for coming here in such an unconventional fashion, when I next see him, but I have acted with the best of intentions, and I don't believe Reverend Solcott would disapprove if he knew. Of course he isn't aware that you take wicked advantage of his goodwill, and make use of his property for the 'most disgraceful goings on whilst he is away.'

'The saintly Gerard?' The thought only seemed to amuse him even more. 'So, you presume to know how my brother would judge my behaviour. That is a little forward, is it not, Miss Bantry, on such a short acquaintance? After all, you've known him less than a week. And siblings can be very close.'

'As a minister of the Church, he would condemn what you are doing,' Virginia said stoutly. 'I am sure he is a good and honest man.'

'And you make a most splendid champion, one of whom I'm sure he would be proud.' The laughter fled from his face. 'But I am being a poor host. Come, let us find a more comfortable place for our conversation.' Placing a hand upon her arm, he led her to the stairs.

His grip was firm but not tight; Virginia thought of pulling free, and instantly abandoned the idea. She wouldn't let this odious man see how scared she was. Despite her appearance, if she remained calm it might be possible to extricate herself from this situation with some shreds of dignity intact.

The man took her into the room she remembered as Mrs Brand's favourite salon; it had a neglected look, but the remains of a fire still smouldered in the grate. He ushered her ceremoniously into a chair by the hearth, stirred up the embers and lit some lamps.

'Now we can act as civilized people, for a little while at least,' he said lightly, taking the seat opposite hers and smiling again.

Virginia saw him clearly for the first time. She gasped. Everything about the man was familiar;

but for his attire, which was in the height of fashion, she would have thought that Reverend Solcott sat before her. He met her astonished gaze with a quizzical look. 'Is something wrong, Miss Bantry?'

'I had not expected you to look so much like your brother,' she said, unable to bide her confusion.

He shrugged his shoulders. 'Ah well, if I had more leisure I suppose I could tell you we were twins. I could weave a tale of Esau and Jacob, but it would be no more than a foolish game. I shan't dissemble, although I admit it is tempting. There is no brother, Miss Bantry. Only myself.'

'I don't understand.'

His lips formed a rueful smile, but there was an expression in his light eyes that she found discomforting. 'Allow me to explain. Reverend Gerard Solcott died some years ago, of natural causes, I must add, in case you were about to lay the blame for his death at my door, along with all my other iniquities. All I did was borrow the man's identity, since it suited my purposes for a while. When his boorish holiness cramps my style, and I tire of wearing black, I can become Gabriel, Gerard's rather dashing younger brother, and sadly, his *bête noir*. That of course, accounts for the two never being seen together. Gabriel is pure invention, since the Reverend Gerard was an only child. I chose the name on a whim; an unfortunate choice perhaps, for I fear the young man has no angelic qualities.'

Virginia's heart seemed to plummet within her, and she could feel it beating hard against her ribs. This deception was far beyond anything she

189

had imagined; she stared into the cheerful features, that disarming face, recalling the sermon he had preached a few days before.

The man was untroubled by her scrutiny. He leant forward to put some more coal on the fire. 'Should I be flattered by so much attention?' he asked.

'How can a man of God be so cruel?' she whispered at last. 'I know what it is that you do. I know that you condemn children to the gross appetites of evil men, to unspeakable horrors...' Her voice faded away.

'To something that is never mentioned in polite society,' he said, 'and yet it is a reality, Miss Bantry, one that has existed for as long as man has walked this earth, and it will go on just as long as he continues to do so. I supply goods, for which there is a demand. If I didn't do so, then there are plenty more to take my place. I confess, I find it refreshing to encounter a young woman who can bear to speak of the sexual act, even if you are mealy-mouthed on the subject.' He flicked an imaginary speck of dust from the embroidered cuff of his jacket. 'As for being a man of the cloth, I regret never having taken Holy Orders. I preach very well, don't you think?'

'You are wholly wicked,' Virginia cried indignantly. 'How can you sit there and admit to such things?'

'Quite easily,' he replied, 'As long as I can do so without consequences to myself. I was fortunate enough to be born without a conscience. Believe me, it makes life a great deal simpler. Besides, I am about to move on; nosy servants and curious neighbours are the very curse of my business, and I find I must take a trip overseas, for the sake of my health, so what you and your sanctimonious friends think of me is of absolutely no account. I had hoped to stay a little longer, but no matter. A boat awaits me, and there are three neat little packages upstairs, all ready for delivery; they should provide sufficient funds to set me up elsewhere, and I do enjoy a sea voyage.

'But now I have you to consider, Miss Bantry.' His gaze searched her features, then ran down to linger on the swell of her breasts, where the loose jacket of her disguise had fallen open. 'You are too old for my usual market, though extremely desirable. And yet – an English rose, beautiful and refined, and undoubtedly a virgin. Even your name makes you more alluring a prospect, dear Virginia. So very apt. I have never turned my back on an opportunity, and here I am, in possession of a rare treasure.'

'I am no man's possession,' she declared, making a valiant attempt to hide her fear.

The man she had known as Solcott leant back in his chair, a look of mock sorrow on his face. 'What would you have me do? I can't deal in such goods in this country, but there is a man in Morocco who will pay handsomely for a woman of your looks and breeding. Luckily I have engaged a boat entirely for my own use, so we can be quite private on our voyage.'

'You wouldn't dare!' She leapt to her feet and turned to run, but he was too quick for her. His hand clamped around her wrist before she had gone a step, and he pulled her back to him. Virginia brought her hand up, attempting to hit him; with a vicious laugh, anticipating her, he lifted his free hand and slapped her across the face.

For a full second Virginia was too shocked to respond; the blow had been hard enough to make her senses reel, but anger overcame her fear. She tried to kick at his legs, but he merely tugged hard at her arm, pulling her off balance. Sobbing in fury and frustration, she clawed left-handed at his cheek, but here too he forestalled her, whirling her around in his grasp so he was behind her. With disconcerting ease, he pinned her arms to her sides.

'Little girls must learn to obey,' he said softly, his breath hot on the side of her neck. 'It is a shame you are valuable, or I'd tame you myself. I could make you blush and shrink and tremble without so much as touching you, Virginia, and that would only be the start of your education. Do you know how easy it is for a woman to become a whore? I could teach you to beg for my attentions, to throw yourself at me, body and soul; this prim little virgin would become no more than a bad memory.' She strained to get away from the damp soft touch of his mouth upon the flesh at her throat, and a shudder passed through her.

'What, don't you like me yet? It takes a little time.' He turned her around again, and she was powerless against him. With a hand circling each wrist, he pressed her to the wall beside the fireplace. 'I am a civilized English gentleman, Virginia, you should be grateful for my forbearance. Months from now you'll look back on this moment and wish you'd been a little kinder. Who knows, if you employed your feminine wiles, perhaps I might be persuaded to keep you as my very own little concubine. Better the devil you know, so they say.'

She squirmed her head aside as his mouth sought hers. Struggle as she might, she couldn't hold him off; his lips and tongue were hot upon her cheeks and her throat, and all the while his eyes were fixed on hers in a greedy scrutiny, as if taking delight in her desperate helplessness. Making a sound more animal than human he came finally to her mouth. His lips felt as hard and unyielding as the fingers that gripped ever tighter about her arms, and he was forcing her lips open, bruising them mercilessly.

With a ferocity she didn't know she possessed, Virginia bit him, clamping her teeth together with all her strength.

'You little wildcat!' He flung her from him, his hands to his mouth. She reeled, almost falling into the fire, her arms flailing as she regained her balance. Not wasting her brief advantage, she recovered swiftly and darted away. She was half-way to the door when it was flung open, to reveal a huge shape looming directly in her path.

Taken by surprise, Mudd simply gawked at her, but her small chance of escape had gone. She dodged back, looking for some other way, but there was none. Solcott, one hand feeling his bloody lip, stared at her as she stood at bay, dishevelled and breathless, her chin tilted in a brave show of defiance.

'Gor blimey,' Mudd said, breaking some strange spell between them. 'Where'd she come from?'

'The cellar, you fool. I told you she might walk

into our trap. Why else do you think I ordered you to leave the door unlocked? Miss Bantry will be travelling with us tomorrow, but we need to find her a safe place for the rest of the night.'

Mudd jerked his head towards the door. 'I c'n put 'er wiv the others.'

'I think not, she has a little more spirit than our normal merchandise, I'd hate to see her climb out of the window and onto the roof. Just imagine what the neighbours would say.'

Solcott looked at the clock on the mantel before turning to Virginia again, his anger evidently forgotten. 'Four hours. That should give you plenty of time to reflect on your future. I think we should make your last morning in England especially memorable, Miss Bantry.' He licked thoughtfully at his lip, which was still bleeding freely. 'I wish I had time to continue our discussion, but we will have plenty of opportunity to get to know each other better while we are at sea. Mudd, fetch some rope, and bring her down to the cellar.'

Simon Roper had given up his search of the mews, for now there was something more urgent to occupy his mind. Cursing under his breath, he climbed over the wall at the back of the end house in Lucas Place, looking for some way to force an entry, but every window had shutters closed tight across it. Flinging himself over the wall once more, he ran past the mews and round to the front, where he skulked down the same basement steps as before. Things looked no better from here; the shutters were closed here too, on the ground floor, and the upper windows were closed. Any attempt to break in here would have to be made in full view of the street.

One thing gave him small comfort: Virginia could not have been removed; even if there had been time, he was satisfied that no carriage had come to take her away.

As he stared at the house, Simon realized that there was a change since he had stood here before; a lamp shone from a room on the second floor. Shadows moved within, as if people were passing rapidly in front of the light, and he had the impression that there was some considerable activity going on in the room. Shortly after, the light dimmed, the room appearing to be lit only by the flickering flames of a fire.

As Simon stood hesitating, a tall man, very upright but silent of tread, entered Lucas Place from the other end, to vanish into the shrubbery that stood at its centre. Recognizing Sergeant Beddowes, Simon shrank lower down the steps. He listened to the murmur of voices, unable to make out what was said. After a minute, somebody emerged from the gloom and began walking away, but it wasn't the sergeant; this was a shorter and more stocky figure.

Beddowes was a natural ally, a police detective who knew all about Miss Bantry, yet Simon couldn't go to him for help; the man had ordered him to return home only seconds before they parted. Simon had made no reply, but seeming to suspect him of having other plans, Beddowes had threatened to send him back to his uncle under police guard if he was found anywhere near Lucas Place.

Careful not to be seen, Simon worked his way back to the garden behind number four. This time he crept closer to the house, pushing past shrubs and stepping through flowerbeds, until he was right up against the rear wall. Not far from the kitchen door was a set of steps leading down into a sunken passage. Wondering if it led to a basement, and a possible weak spot, Simon felt his way cautiously down the stairs, to peer in through the dirt-specked window at the bottom.

As he put a hand upon the grimy window sill, Simon knew he had been here before, on this very spot. It took a moment longer to work out that this was where he had stood, only seconds before Mudd had crept up and hit him from behind. Whirling round, fist raised and heart pounding, Simon glared into the gloom that surrounded him. Nobody stood in the shadows, or lurked amongst the bushes that straggled above the steps.

Feeling a little foolish, Simon relaxed his hand and continued his exploration. Some instinct led him to a sloping wooden hatch. With bewildering abruptness, perhaps revived by the dank smell of mould and the faint tick of dripping water, the memory of that night came back to him with crystal clarity. Mudd hadn't carried him into the cellar by way of the stairs. He had tipped him down the chute, like a sack of coal.

Chapter Eighteen

'Quiet, ain't she?' Mudd said, as he slid Virginia off his shoulder and onto the stone floor. 'Not like that ol' cow you 'ad me bury under the midden. I fort that ol' bag would never stop screechin'.'

'Yes, well, we were mere amateurs then, and we hadn't discovered our very own disposal system down here,' Solcott replied. He pulled Virginia to her feet. 'You must have seen our pleasant little stream when you came to the rescue of young Roper.' He smiled at her, his expression one of benign indulgence. 'I wouldn't like you to think you'd outsmarted me; it didn't take long to work out where he'd gone, and that he'd had help. There was nobody at the mews who would dare risk upsetting Mudd by betraying us, so we knew that route was safe, and the old madman next door had the entrance to his cellar blocked up years ago. As for the two ancient hags, they are renowned for their fear of the bogeyman who lurks below ground, or some such nonsense. That left me with only one suspect; I knew I was looking for some-body in the famous Sir Mortimer's household.

'Since Mudd had some acquaintance with Sir Mortimer's butler, and had gained some idea of the establishment, it didn't take long to work out that I had been visited by the charming Miss Bantry. One day you must entertain me with the whole story, I would love to know what motive you had for breaking into my cellar in the middle of the night. I doubt if you expected to encounter your charming young Romeo. You see, I know it all. I was in the park when you had your romantic little tête-à-tête.'

'You can't have been,' Virginia said, 'we would have seen you.'

'I assure you I was there. Once I leave off my clerical drab and put on frock coat and silk hat, only the most astute observer would recognize me. Besides, you were so very wrapped up in one another.'

'Then you know that Mr Roper is sure to look for me,' Virginia shot back, 'and he won't be alone. My cousin arrives in London this morning, and he won't rest until I am found. You would be well advised to let me go now, along with those poor girls you have locked in your attic. If you hurry you might still be able to escape.'

Solcott laughed. 'Such arrogant assurance. Dear Virginia, I find you very entertaining. I'm sorry to disappoint you, but you won't be rid of me so easily, I'm afraid I couldn't bear to lose your company. As for your hero, it seems a shame, after you rescued him so very gallantly, but he won't be returning the favour. It was unwise of him to meddle in my business, and he's about to pay the price. We had a message, not ten minutes before you arrived; it seems Mr Roper has been awaiting our pleasure these past six hours, thanks to the efforts of a gentleman by the name of Higgs. Once you are safely settled for the rest of the night, Mudd will go and finish what he started in the cellar last week, and rid me of Mr Roper permanently.'

'I don't believe you,' she shot back, 'but even if what you say is true, there is still my cousin.'

'Yes, the esteemed Sir Mortimer. Think about it, Virginia. When you and young Roper are discovered to have vanished at the same time, your cousin, and the rest of London, will conclude that two silly young fools eloped, rather than wait and gain their families' approval for a match. It could be weeks before the truth is discovered, if ever, and by then you'll be wearing a silken veil in a certain Moroccan harem, and young Roper will be no more than a scattering of bones at the bottom of the sea.'

'No!' Virginia launched herself at him, her fingers clawing at his mocking eyes, but Mudd's huge arms encircled her waist and she was lifted from the ground, her body squeezed until she cried out in pain.

'Put her against the pillar, Mudd.' Solcott was already tying a rope around one of her wrists. 'I'm sorry not to be able to offer you a chair, my dear girl, but I rather think that's your own fault.' She could do nothing to prevent them from dragging her arms behind her and around the column in an uncomfortable embrace.

'Mudd,' Solcott said suddenly, 'go and make sure we'll be having no more uninvited guests. We've caught our little intruder, and I think it's time we closed our doors.' With a nod the big man knocked out more bricks to enlarge the gap in the wall, squeezed through and vanished from sight. Solcott turned back to Virginia and checked the ropes to make sure she couldn't free herself. There was no need to do more, for their treatment had rendered her helpless, but with an unpleasant smile on his lips, the man began wrapping more of the rope around her body, his hands lingering over the task as he touched her breasts and hips, until he was caressing her in the most loathsome way. Virginia bit her lip and held her peace, knowing that revealing her fear and revulsion would only gratify him.

She couldn't help recalling the warmth of the sensations she had enjoyed at the slightest brush of Simon's skin upon hers; they had made her feel a little wicked, but it had been a wholly pleasurable experience. The hands of this man made her feel dirty; she was sure a week of scrubbing at her abused flesh would never remove the foulness of his touch.

Mudd returned, leering at Virginia as he came to hand something to his master. Solcott dropped the object into his fob pocket and stepped back to look at her; she was bound so tightly by this time that she could barely move a muscle. 'You will find that quite painful in time,' her tormentor said conversationally. 'When I return perhaps you will be a little more appreciative of my company.' He bent to pick up the lamp he had brought with him. 'And you won't need this. Sleep well, Virginia.'

'Wait,' she called, as he followed Mudd up the steps. She was unable to keep her voice from quivering a little. The thought of darkness was suddenly unbearable. 'Please, if you have any humanity left in you, leave me a candle at least.'

'Oh dear, you are still under the mistaken belief that I am a man of God. I already told you, Virginia, I have no conscience.' He turned to look down at her, his hand going to his swollen lip. 'You should bear in mind that I don't forgive easily, either. If you weren't worth a good deal of money you'd have been dropped down to old Father Thames, or into a hole in the garden like Mrs Ross.' The now familiar smile, first seen in church and almost saintly in its benignity, appeared on his face with its usual disconcerting suddenness. 'But then again, you are so very beautiful. I have rarely been so tempted to sample my own merchandise.'

The door closed with a thud, and she was alone, blind and terrified in the dark. Fear overcoming her, Virginia screamed. Her voice resounded across the empty chamber. Despite the echo, it was a dead sound. Nobody would hear. Very soon her cries became whimpers and sank into silence. She was buried just as securely as Mrs Ross, the poor housekeeper having evidently been thrust unceremoniously into a hole in the garden, presumably for being too interested in the new tenant's affairs.

Anger came to her rescue, and pride; she was first cousin to Sir Mortimer Bantry, the man who had once tricked his way out of the hands of cannibals with nothing more than a broken pistol and a compass to aid him. The same spirit dwelt within her, the same blood flowed through her veins; she would not give up hope so soon. Solcott was a devil, and while she lived she would defy him.

To distract herself from the growing pain in her cramped body, she began to consider her chances of being rescued. She daren't think too much of Simon, that way led to despair.

She turned instead to considering Willshire, and

201

Emily; the poor girl was still in Solcott's house, but she was due to be spirited away very soon, and even if Virginia could escape in time to save herself from disgrace, it was likely to be too late for the little maid. It was hard to believe that Willshire was in league with such wicked men, but she had seen the evidence with her own eyes. What would he do when the household awoke in the morning to find that she had vanished? Would Cook recall that Virginia had intended the girl for better things than the position of kitchen maid? Solcott was right: if she and Simon both disappeared at once, never to be seen again, people would assume that they had eloped, running away together rather than waiting to obtain Sir Mortimer's blessing, and it would be easy for Willshire to add credence to that lie. Perhaps he would even suggest that Emily had been taken to act as Virginia's servant, to give some respectability to the affair.

Virginia vowed that she would escape; she couldn't let any blame fall on Simon. Let it be a lie that he was a prisoner again; let him still be free! But Solcott had sounded so sure of himself. She prayed then, with every fibre of her being, more earnestly than she had ever prayed in her whole life, but all around her was nothing but the dark, dank silence, and in time tears began to run hotly down her cheeks. Her voice rose again to a shrill wail, and as her heart and lungs strained, the ropes that bound her dug ever deeper into her flesh until she drooped in exhaustion, her sobs giving way to small hiccups of misery.

Sergeant Beddowes stood like a statue; during his

ten years as a soldier he had perfected the art of being still. His whole attention was focused on number four, Lucas Place; he stared intensely at the house, as if with sufficient effort he could see his suspects through the walls. He was uneasy; but for that young fool Roper, Beddowes reflected, he would have remained on surveillance duty all night. Being tipped the wink that Roper had been nabbed by Higgs, he could trust nobody else to set the boy free without arousing his captor's suspicions, and before Mudd could be located by Higgs's messenger. He was confident of his own cover, having worked hard at it for six months; he had acted the itinerant ex-soldier to perfection, and had no fears of Mudd seeing through his disguise.

The officer sighed; this case wasn't proceeding to Inspector Laker's plan. Shortly before his return to Lucas Place, the man watching the mews and the rear entrance of the house had been drawn from his post by screams and shouts of 'murder' in the next street, only to find nothing amiss when he arrived, breathless, at the scene. An uncomfortable itch between his shoulders told Beddowes that Mudd had arranged the incident as a diversion, perhaps to allow Solcott to reach the house unseen. Mudd had a secret way in and out, that much he knew, and there was no reason to think his master wouldn't use it, especially now, when he could have been warned that his operation was at risk.

The chime of the nearest church clock told Beddowes that half an hour had passed since his arrival. All the houses in Lucas Place looked dark and lifeless, apart from the dim glow of a lamp in the sickroom where old Mr Parkin lay. His ears registered distant sounds, a rumble as a heavy cart passed along the high road, small rustlings in the bushes, and then, more interestingly, a faint thud that he recognized; there was a loose paving slab just round the corner in Newscombe Street. Somebody was coming.

Mudd barrelled round the corner, head down and hunched so his bull-like shoulders appeared to lead the way. He walked straight past the hidden Beddowes, and the policeman watched until he was beyond the end of the street, then darted from his lair and hurried after him. There might be trouble, since he was abandoning the inspector's careful plan, but instinct told him that time was running out, and this was an opportunity not to be missed; it would be far easier to deal with Mudd while he was separated from his master, and not on his own home territory. Reaching the end of the street where he'd be out of sight from the house, Beddowes raised one arm in the prearranged signal, and at once two more figures came oozing from the shadows to join him in his pursuit.

Exhausted, Virginia had sunk into total silence. The pain from the ropes was too much of a torment to allow her to sleep; every part of her body was protesting; she had never realized how important it was to be able to move. From some distant corner came a rasp, like the scrape of wood on stone; it reminded her of the sound of Simon's chair being dragged across the cellar floor by Solcott. That night seemed a lifetime ago.

During all her visits to the cellars Virginia had refused to believe in ghosts, but now, alone, hurting and abandoned in the dark, a new horror engulfed her. Her lips parted in a prayer, but no suitable words of supplication came, only a rending heartfelt plea, uttered with all the power she had left within her. 'Simon!'

Against all probability, a reply came, but not in Simon's longed-for voice. Instead, a strange hollow whisper spoke her name; the sound reverberated from the stones, coming to her from every direction at once. 'Virginia?'

She couldn't help herself. She screamed, long and loud. There was another scraping sound, louder this time, followed by an echoing thud and a yelp of pain. 'Virginia?'

It was hard to find the breath to speak. 'Simon? You're here!'

'I'm here. But where are you?'

She could hear him stumbling in the dark. 'Here. I'm here, against the pillar.'

'I can't see the pillars – ouch, I can feel them though. Keep talking to me, I'll try to follow your voice, but the echo makes it difficult.'

'You're getting nearer, I'm sure of it. This way, I'm right here. Was that you saying my name? You frightened me. It sounded as if you were speaking from the bottom of a well.'

'More like the top. Sorry. I came down the coal chute. Keep talking.'

'Simon, Simon, Simon.' She repeated his name like a mantra, calling him to her, all her hurts and fears forgotten. 'I thought I'd never see you again.'

'We're not exactly seeing each other,' he said, laughter in his voice, as his fingers encountered the collar of her jacket. 'Whatever are you wearing?'

'Never mind that, see if you can untie me.'

'Did Mudd do this?' he asked furiously, as he ran tentative fingers down her arms.

'No, it was Solcott. Can't you find the knots?'

'It would be easier if I had a light. Oh, my poor love, its so tight.'

'It doesn't matter, not now you're here. Wait, there's a candle tucked inside my shirt, and a matchbox. They slipped down to my waist when Mudd threw me on the floor. See if you can reach them.'

After Solcott's attentions, Virginia had been uncertain how she would feel about being touched by a man's hand, but as Simon's fingers quested tentatively with the buttons of her jacket she smiled widely in the darkness, hot tears starting in her eyes. 'There's no need to be so careful, Simon,' she scolded, picturing the flush that would be rising to his cheeks, the thought bringing her close to both laughter and tears. 'I won't break. We don't have time for you to be bashful.'

By way of reply he withdrew his hand, felt in the darkness for her cheek, laying his hand against it. With a fierce kind of care, he placed his lips upon hers and kissed her, long and hard.

A long moment later, breathless and without waiting for her to speak, he resumed his search, and soon there came the scrape of a match. The candle had broken into three, but one piece which had a good length of wick was lit and set

206

upon the floor. Rescued and rescuer stared upon each other, two pairs of eyes wide, a whole world of emotions in the look they shared.

'I hadn't expected to need this again,' Simon muttered, taking the broken knife from his pocket, 'but it will be quicker than undoing knots with one hand.'

'As quick as you can,' she urged. 'I don't know how soon they'll be back.'

'It's taken me so long to find a way in. I saw you with Willshire, I could hardly believe it when I saw the rogue handing you over to Mudd. But for my hand I'd have tried to do something there and then, though the brutes probably would have been too much for me.'

'Willshire? But that wasn't me!'

He paused in his task to stare at her. 'I recognized your coat!'

'It was Emily, our kitchen maid. I've never liked Willshire, but to surrender a poor harmless little thing like Emily to Mudd, I could hardly believe it! Why would he do such a thing?'

'I overheard him talking to the man who owns the mews,' Simon said, sawing with the knife again. 'It sounded as if he had gambling debts. Maybe they threatened him with Mudd if he didn't find some way to repay them. So you saw Willshire and this girl. Did you discover how to get out by the mews?'

'No, I was too far behind them, so I came through the cellars. You see, I'd met Mr Jeffrey Parkin during the afternoon, and he told me that since he came home he sometimes heard people crying in the attic. I guessed that was where

Emily would be taken, and I decided to try to rescue her. I found the door into the house open, and I went to look, but Solcott found me.'

'And brought you back down here.' He grimaced. 'You were lucky they didn't drop you straight into the river.'

'They talked about it. And oh, Simon, they killed the poor housekeeper and buried her out in the garden.'

'Let's be thankful they daren't do the same to Miss Virginia Bantry.'

It was her turn to blush. 'They were going to sell me to a man in Morocco.'

Simon chewed on his lip as he worked, but he said nothing.

'Aren't you going to scold me?' she asked, in a small meek voice. 'I know I shouldn't have come here. And after all you said.'

'I wasn't thinking about that, only about how I can get my hands on Solcott while his tame ape is out of the way. I'll scold you properly, once we're out of here and you're safe. Keep still just a bit longer, I don't want to cut you.'

Within minutes she was in his arms, clinging to him. He eased himself from her grasp. 'We don't have time for this. Can you stand?' She nodded, and he left her, running back through the chamber and up the steps.

'What are you doing?' she called. 'We can't go that way.'

'I hoped there might be a bolt on this side, or some way to slow them down, but no luck.' Simon hurried back to her, where she stood chafing life into her limbs. 'It would have been nice to have another escape route, too, just in case. Are you well enough to move?'

She nodded, taking a hold on his arm. 'The sooner the better.'

They climbed through the gap in the wall, the stub of candle flickering, only to come to a dismayed halt a few yards further on.

'But I came this way!' Virginia said despairingly. Instead of the old wooden door, crumbling away to dust, a new one stood in their path, and it was locked.

Chapter Nineteen

'You sure about this, Sergeant?' the constable asked Beddowes, as, flanked by the other two officers, he closed in on Mudd. At bay, the man looked bigger and more menacing than ever, and there was a smile on his face that didn't bode well for the police officers.

Beddowes didn't answer the query, but addressed one of his own to their quarry. 'Why don't you come quietly? Resisting arrest will make things worse in the long run.'

The big man spat. 'Bloody rozzers! An' you a bloody sergeant! I should've guessed, the way you kep' gettin' in me way. I c'ld've done you in las' time I knocked you down; a coupla kicks to the 'ead, an' nobody the wiser! Still, 'ere you are, so it ain't too late.'

'In view of that last meeting of ours, maybe this

is best after all,' Beddowes replied. 'Come on then, lads, we'll do it his way.' With that he launched himself at Mudd, and was relieved to see his men move with him, their truncheons at the ready. The affair would have been settled quicker if Inspector Laker had applied to the superintendent to get hold of a couple of pistols, he reflected wryly.

The attack went badly from the start. As Beddowes ploughed in, feinting left in an attempt to grab Mudd's deadly right arm as it swung for his ribs, the constable at his side tripped, pushing him off balance. Mudd's blow caught Beddowes on the cheek, and he fell, with blood in his mouth and his head ringing.

Buoyed up by this success and uttering a mighty roar of defiance, Mudd downed the second man with his left; the constable dropped like a felled tree and didn't get up again. The only policeman still on his feet dropped back a step, circling warily.

Beddowes rose, shaking his head. He slipped a hand into his pocket and brought out a long thin object which jingled slightly as he swung it in the air. Darting behind Mudd as he made a lunge at the constable, the sergeant moved in, bringing the makeshift cosh down at the bottom of Mudd's skull.

Instead of dropping under the blow, the giant didn't even falter. Having downed his other opponent he turned on Beddowes, with fury in his eyes and murder in his heart. His enormous right hand opened up, powerful fingers reaching to take the sergeant's neck in a fearsome grip. Beddowes was hurled backwards by Mudd's assault. He punched intermittently at the huge face looming over him, but he was losing the fight; Mudd didn't loosen his hold, and the sergeant's face was turning purple, his breath coming in short hard gasps that grew ever weaker. The constable was getting groggily to his feet, but it looked as if he'd be too late.

The copper-filled bag was still in Beddowes's hand, but there was no room to get in a decent blow. With a grunt he swung the heavy roll of canvas over his knuckles, his little finger taking a precarious grip on the other end, then with every ounce of strength that was left to him, the sergeant sent his fist smashing into Mudd's face, right between the eyes.

Blood spraying from his nose and eyes, Mudd staggered backwards then fell. The constable was instantly upon him, with handcuffs ready in his fist. These were fastened to Mudd's wrists with trembling alacrity, but the big man was finished for the time being, his bloodshot eyes turned up in his head, and a heavy snore issuing from his mouth.

'Looks like you might've done for him, Sergeant.'

'And good riddance,' Beddowes said hoarsely, massaging his throat as he came to stare down at the defeated colossus. 'He'll have had worse in the ring, I daresay he'll live.' He winced, cradling his right hand. 'I'll shed no tears either way, it feels like my hand's broken. You all right, Dobbs?' he queried, looking over at the other constable, who was just rising to his knees.

'I'll do, Sergeant,' Dobbs replied.

'Good,' Beddowes nodded. 'Piper, nip down to the nearest station and fetch the local lads; see if you can get Mudd tucked away before the word gets around, and then you'd better report to Inspector Laker. Tell him I'll be going back to Lucas Place, we don't want the big fish getting away.'

'If that was the tiddler, I don't fancy tryin' to catch the big 'un,' Piper commented, as he hurried off.

'They were expecting you,' Simon said, staring helplessly at the locked door. 'They must have fastened this after you came through.'

She nodded. 'He sent Mudd to do it, I remember now. I thought I'd been so clever,' she added bitterly, 'but I didn't even notice they'd put in a new door. What can we do?'

'There has to be another way.'

It didn't take long to discover he was wrong. Peering into every corner, holding the candle up in the hope that it would locate some draught of air, they found nothing.

'The coal chute,' Virginia said suddenly, 'can't we climb back up there?'

He shook his head. 'We couldn't reach it, there's a drop of a dozen feet or more. We're trapped until somebody lets us out, and that's likely to be Mudd and Solcott. I'm sorry, I didn't think before I came down, but once I'd heard you, what else could I do?'

'Nothing,' Virginia said. She smiled, the sparkle of tears in her eyes. 'I am so glad you're here. I couldn't wish for anything better.' Reaching up, she placed a kiss upon his mouth. When he

212

recoiled she stared questioningly into his eyes. 'I want more from you than a kiss, Simon. I've been dreaming of lying in your arms ever since that night. Do you think I'm brazen?

'I don't know what to think. You–' She silenced him with another kiss, then released him and turned away.

'Solcott means to sell me.' Virginia said.

'I'll kill him first,' Simon broke in fiercely. 'There must be some way–'

'–to defeat both Mudd and Solcott?' she queried. 'Simon, listen. We only have an hour or two. I think I'd prefer death to what Solcott has planned for me, but if I live, then I shall soon know far too much about lust, and cruelty, like those poor children you and your uncle set out to save. Show me what love means, Simon. Show me the best that can happen between a man and a woman, before I'm forced to learn about the worst.'

'Virginia, you know how I feel about you. But your reputation–'

She gave a tremulous laugh. '–will be ruined within a day, whatever happens now. Ever since that night, you've been all I can think of, and those thoughts and feelings may be sinful, but I don't care. You know what I'm asking, but I beg you don't make me put it into words, because I hardly know what they are.'

'I love you so much,' he said, enfolding her. 'I was planning to be on your doorstep in a few hours, to ask your cousin's permission to marry you. I couldn't bear to waste a day.'

'But we don't have a day, just an hour, if our

luck holds that long.'

'There might still be something we can do. Perhaps we can barricade the hole in the wall, fight them off.'

'Will you refuse the one thing I've ever asked of you?' she demanded, lifting her face so he could see the tears running down her cheeks. 'Life or death, wherever I'm going, let me have one good memory to take with me. Please.'

Very gently he lifted her left hand, and kissed the third finger. 'I have no ring, only a promise. Virginia Bantry, before God, and with all my heart, I take you for my wife, in sickness and in health, until death parts us. I swear I shall do all I can to keep you from harm, or die trying.' Awkward with his injured fingers, somehow he lifted her, and laid her down on the dusty floor. He tore off his clothes, to make a place for her to lie.

Her eyes wide in the flickering light of the candle, Virginia lay still as he unfastened the shirt she wore, and then, his touch a little tremulous, removed the boots and breeches. Simon exclaimed angrily over the bruises that marred her pale flesh.

'Hush.' She lifted her body so he could release her from her underclothes. 'Simon,' she whispered. 'My husband.' Very gently, his fingers touched her hurts, as if he might wipe them away, and without conscious thought she responded, revelling once again in the throbbing heat that rose from deep within her. His lips caressed her face, her lips, her neck, soft yet urgent. As they moved to savour her breasts she moaned a little, her body moving of its own volition; it ached to

214

bring him closer. His hand was on her belly now, feeling its way to the fire his touch had lit. Abruptly, shamelessly, she pulled him down to her; if this was sin then she was lost, for she had never felt so fully alive before.

The stub of candle guttered and died, but they didn't notice; lost in each other, far beyond redemption, they needed no light to see their way.

'Was it necessary to render Mudd unconscious?' Inspector Laker asked testily. He stood beside Sergeant Beddowes in the shadows at the entrance to Lucas Place, his eyes fixed on the last house as the first light of dawn appeared. 'Mr Roper will be here any minute, hoping for news of his nephew, but I gather it could be hours before the man is fit to talk.'

'I'm sorry, sir,' Beddowes said woodenly. 'Couldn't be helped.' His apology was insincere, for his hand had swollen hugely and his throat was still sore. 'This'll be Mr Roper now, Inspector.'

A long-legged figure joined them, offering a hurried greeting. 'Best we don't go too close, Mr Roper,' Laker said, 'we don't want him to know we're here, not just yet.'

'You've no news of my nephew?' Jocelyn asked.

'Nothing certain, but there was some talk of a man climbing over the garden wall during the night. I think we must assume young Mr Roper got inside the house somehow. You don't need to worry; we have the whole area cordoned off.'

'That's right, sir,' Sergeant Beddowes added. 'Whichever burrow our weasel chooses to pop

215

out of, we'll be ready for him. There's men in the mews, as well as here and in Newscombe Street. If he's there our villain won't get away.'

'What happened to your hand, Sergeant?' Jocelyn looked concerned. 'Shouldn't that be tended?'

'Just a run-in with Mudd, sir,' Beddowes replied. 'It can wait.'

'That man seems to specialize in broken fingers.'

'Oh, he's not fussy, sir,' the sergeant said. 'Noses, heads, legs, fingers, it's all the same to him. As a matter of fact this was my own fault. Something a bit hard got between his head and my fist, you might say.'

'Can't you act now?' Jocelyn was shivering, although the morning wasn't particularly cold. 'You say you have evidence against Solcott, can't you go in and fetch the man out?'

'Best if he comes to us,' Laker said. 'I'd like to take him red-handed, it makes things so much easier in the long run; we hope there's merchandise in the house, but we can't be sure. Thanks to the sergeant here, we can't get a word out of Mudd. If our villain doesn't show himself within the hour, though, I'll try knocking at the door. No need for you to stay, I can send a messenger the moment there's news.'

Jocelyn Roper shook his head and shrugged his shoulders into his coat; deeper lines etched themselves into his thin features as he settled down to wait. He cared not a fig for Solcott; the man could walk free as long as Simon was alive and well.

A match flared in the dark, and Virginia blinked at the sudden light. 'I'm sorry,' Simon said, 'but we need to get ready. I'll not let the rogues take you without a fight. Let's see what we can find, it will be better than sitting here waiting.' He vanished through the gap in the wall, and she quickly gathered up her clothes, retreating further into the shadows to dress, her face and neck hot. What had happened between them had seemed inevitable, and completely right; nothing would change that, yet she was horribly aware that the rest of the world would see things differently.

She found him gathering the pieces of rope that had bound her to the pillar. He ran up the stairs with them, but soon returned, shaking his head. 'I was hoping to fix the door, or trip them on the stairs, but I can't see any way of doing it. That leaves us the bricks.'

'It's no use trying to rebuild the wall, Mudd would only push it down.'

'I wasn't bad at cricket when I was at school. I've never tried throwing a brick, but it can't be too difficult. Maybe I'll get lucky and knock them out as they try to climb through into the other cellar. I'll gather all the ammunition on the other side.'

Virginia hurried to help. They had almost finished piling the bricks in a heap when Simon leant over to blow out the candle. 'Somebody's coming,' he whispered.

A faint light moved across the space where they crouched, hidden. A single set of footsteps pounded down the stairs, starting an echo. 'I hope you are feeling fresh and ready to travel, my dear girl,' Solcott said. 'As soon as Mudd returns from dispatching young Roper we'll be–' He broke off. 'How did you do that, you little devil? If you make me play hide and seek you'll be sorry. I can see I'll have to spend more time on discipline. Come out, right now.'

The light flared and wavered as Solcott swung the lamp high. Virginia caught a glimpse of Simon's face; it wore a look she had never thought to see there. She couldn't suppress a shiver, for what she read in his eyes was murder, as naked and unashamed as the love they had shared a short time before.

'I don't know how you got free, Virginia,' Solcott was saying, as he thrust his way into the gap, 'but I'll make you wish–'

Instead of throwing the brick, Simon swung it, with all his strength, into the man's face. Solcott's words were swallowed up by a frightful sound, as flesh and bone shattered, and his mouth filled with blood. A gurgling scream echoed round the cellar. His eyes hard and unfocused, Simon lifted the brick to land another blow, but Virginia caught his arm.

'No,' she said, staring at the ruin of Solcott's face in horror. 'That's enough. I don't want you to kill him, not for me. You don't need to. We have the rope, we can tie him.'

Simon shook himself free. 'He showed you no mercy, Virginia. You heard what he said. You could have died down here in the dark and he wouldn't have cared.'

'We aren't like him,' she said. Solcott had his

hands to his face, and as she threaded a length of rope around his wrists he didn't resist.

'Virginia–' Simon began, but she merely shook her head. 'Very well, if that's what you want. Just make sure you tie it tightly.'

When it was done, they pulled Solcott completely through the gap, leaving him there with his ruined face still bleeding freely.

'We'd better leave before Mudd returns.' Simon swept up the lantern and they ran across to the stairs. The door above stood open, but as they started up the steps a loud banging from within the house brought them to a halt. It sounded as if somebody was trying to knock the front door down.

'He must have locked Mudd out,' Virginia said, shrinking back.

'I don't think so.' Simon took another step upwards. 'I think–'

From outside came a great bellow. 'Open in the name of the law!'

Simon gathered her in his arms and pushed her back the way they had come. 'You'll have to go home this way,' he said breathlessly. 'If only Solcott has the key–'

'He put it in his pocket,' she said. 'But why must I go? Mudd can't hurt us now the police have come.'

'Do you know what you look like? My dear girl, I'd marry you without any sort of reputation, but think of your cousin. What will he say if he comes home to find you dressed as an urchin, and caught up in a house full of villains?'

'But poor Emily, shut away in the attics–'

'I'll look after Emily.' Simon had recovered the key from Solcott's coat and thrust it into the lock before she had time to say more. 'You won't get lost?'

'No. I know the way.'

'You'd better take the lamp.' He was staring down at her with hungry eyes, as if he feared they might never meet again.

She smiled up at him, reaching inside her shirt to take out the matchbox and the last piece of candle. 'No, I don't need it.' Stretching up, she kissed his cheek. 'Come and call on my cousin very soon, or I'll come looking for you.' And with that she left, darting down the dark passageway. She had no idea what the hour might be; she could only pray that the household weren't yet up and about.

There was nobody in the hall, and silence reigned as she crept up the stairs. Softly closing the door of her room, she leant her back against it. Suddenly, inexplicably, she was shaking from head to toe, and she had to thrust her fist in her mouth to keep herself from crying out loud, yet she couldn't begin to know why.

Several shaken minutes later, Virginia threw off the outfit of clothes she had gathered with such dedication; she would never wear them again. Haphazardly flinging them back in the trunk, she made swift preparations for bed, sank down without pulling back the covers, and was instantly asleep.

It was the commotion in the street that woke her; seemingly only minutes had passed although it was full daylight. Virginia's eyes stung with tiredness, but she dragged herself across to the window. A hansom cab was pulling up outside, but it wasn't that which had disturbed her. There were police officers further along the street, facing a small crowd of onlookers who were shouting and jeering at a dishevelled figure with his arms chained behind him, and blood still dripping from his nose, who was being hurried into a black carriage with bars across the window.

Virginia craned to see more, and was rewarded by the sight of three men. The two Ropers, uncle and nephew, stood either side of a portly, well-dressed man, who appeared to be in charge of the proceedings. There was a diminutive figure dressed in an over-long coat clinging to Simon's arm as if she would never let go; Emily was safe.

Close by, the tall man they had suspected of being in league with Mudd, his back ramrod straight, was standing guard over two smaller girls; these two were wrapped in each others' arms, so tightly entwined that it was hard to see where one began and the other ended.

Intent as she was on all this, Virginia hardly noticed the familiar figure in travelling clothes who had descended from the cab; he strode across to join the Ropers, hand outstretched and calling a greeting to his old friend.

Abandoning the window, her weariness forgotten, Virginia flew around the room. She chose a costume at random from her wardrobe and dressed as quickly as she could. Even so, she was still in her room when the doorbell rang, setting foot on the stairs as she heard the bolt on the front door being dragged back. Racing down, she was in time to throw herself into her cousin's arms before he could show his unexpected guests into the morning room.

The publishers hope that this book has given you enjoyable reading. Large Print Books are especially designed to be as easy to see and hold as possible. If you wish a complete list of our books please ask at your local library or write directly to:

Magna Large Print Books
Magna House, Long Preston,
Skipton, North Yorkshire.
BD23 4ND

This Large Print Book for the partially sighted, who cannot read normal print, is published under the auspices of

THE ULVERSCROFT FOUNDATION